"Yuck," Jake said, looking at the squashed pizza.

Berry was intrigued by his mouth. It was probably the greatest mouth she'd ever seen.

"Are you going to kiss me?" he asked suddenly.

"Certainly not!" she said.

"You were staring at my mouth."

"It's a terrific mouth."

He chuckled softly, considering her tangled blonde curls and cornflower blue eyes. "I suppose you're the owner of that jeep—" As he spoke, the aged jeep began rolling slowly backward down the hill. Berry started sprinting after it and had nearly caught it when she was tackled from behind and thrown to the ground.

"Get off me," she yelled. "You must weigh two hundred pounds."

"One-seventy-eight, and it's all muscle."

She already knew that. They were lying zipper to zipper, knee to knee, his chest skimming hers, his delicious mouth hovering inches above her own. Berry felt her body tingling, growing overheated. She was in lust, no doubt about it.

"You're staring at my mouth again," he murmured in a voice that reminded her of fine whiskey and satin teddies.

She wondered if he could feel her heart pounding through her shirt. She could see it in his eyes. He was going to kiss her. . . .

WHAT ARE *LOVESWEPT* ROMANCES?

They are stories of true romance and touching emotion. We believe those two very important ingredients are constants in our highly sensual and very believable stories in the *LOVESWEPT* line. Our goal is to give you, the reader, stories of consistently high quality that may sometimes make you laugh, sometimes make you cry, but are always fresh and creative and contain many delightful surprises within their pages.

Most romance fans read an enormous number of books. Those they truly love, they keep. Others may be traded with friends and soon forgotten. We hope that each *LOVESWEPT* romance will be a treasure—a "keeper." We will always try to publish

LOVE STORIES YOU'LL NEVER FORGET
BY AUTHORS YOU'LL ALWAYS REMEMBER

The Editors

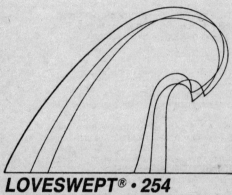

LOVESWEPT® • 254

Janet Evanovich
The Grand Finale

 BANTAM BOOKS
TORONTO • NEW YORK • LONDON • SYDNEY • AUCKLAND

THE GRAND FINALE

A Bantam Book / May 1988

*If you would be interested in receiving protective vinyl
covers for your Loveswept books, please write to this address
for information:*

*Loveswept
Bantam Books
P.O. Box 985
Hicksville, NY 11802*

ISBN 0-553-21893-X

Published simultaneously in the United States and Canada

*Bantam Books are published by Bantam Books, a division
of Bantam Doubleday Dell Publishing Group, Inc. Its trademark, consisting of the words "Bantam Books" and the
portrayal of a rooster, is Registered in U.S. Patent and
Trademark Office and in other countries. Marca Registrada.
Bantam Books, 666 Fifth Avenue, New York, New York 10103.*

PRINTED IN THE UNITED STATES OF AMERICA

O   0 9 8 7 6 5 4 3 2 1

One

Berry Knudsen eased her battered army surplus jeep over to the curb, pulled the emergency brake on, and studied the only mailbox in the deserted cul-de-sac. No name. No street number. *Terrific.* She squinted into the blackness and reread the address taped to the large pizza box on the seat next to her. 5077 Ellenburg Drive. This had to be it. This was Ellenburg Drive, and this was the only house for a quarter of a mile. She thunked her forehead onto the steering wheel and groaned. Last delivery of the night, and it had all the earmarks of a prank.

The house was a three-story Victorian perched on a small hillock. A sliver of moon ducked behind the clouds throwing ghostly highlights over the house, and a chill March wind moaned through a giant oak standing guard over the lawn on the south side. Berry grimaced and decided Jack the Ripper would have felt comfy here. Quasimodo could have added a bell tower and been happy as a clam at high tide. And Count Dracula . . . Count Dracula would have traded half the blood in Transylvania for a house like this. But it's not in Transylvania, Berry reminded herself. It's in suburban Seattle and probably belongs to some nice little old lady and her nephew . . . Norman.

She grimly noted that there wasn't a light shining anywhere. No car in the driveway. No sign of life that might require a large pizza with the works. Damn. I should go up and ring the doorbell, she thought, but who knows what lurks on the other side of that ornate, handcarved front door—could be some pervert, sitting in the dark in his undershorts, waiting for the pizza delivery lady.

Berry pushed her short, blonde curls behind her ear. That's ridiculous, she told herself. Lord, how did she come up with these ideas? Mr. Large Pizza with the Works simply wasn't home. He probably went out for a six-pack of beer. Happened all the time. And since he wasn't home . . . there certainly wasn't any reason why she should go up and ring the doorbell. What she should do is get her fanny the heck out of this creepy cul-de-sac.

She was startled by a small sound that raised the hairs on her neck and caused beads of sweat to pop out on her upper lip. Some creature whined high in the oak tree—a pathetic little meow, filled with fear and wavering uncertainty. Berry closed her eyes in relief and slumped in her seat when she realized it was the call of a kitten. It cried out again, and Berry knew she was doomed. She was a sucker for lost dogs, fallen nestlings, and stranded kittens. She grabbed the pizza box and set off across the lawn, drawing courage from the fact that the Victorian house looked less sinister at close range. It had been freshly painted lemon yellow. The intricate gingerbread trim sported a new coat of white. The windows were curtainless, but the panes reflected a recent cleaning. The cat looked down at Berry and swished its tail.

"Kitty, kitty, kitty," Berry called softly.

"Meow."

Berry bit her lower lip. The dumb cat was stuck in the tree. A blast of wind ruffled the kitten's fur, causing the little ball of fluff to huddle closer to the limb. Berry rolled her eyes and plunked the pizza box on the ground beside the tree. "Don't get me wrong," she mumbled to the cat as she scrambled to shinny up the tree. "It isn't as if I don't like kittens. And it isn't that I mind climbing trees. It's just that I've about filled my good deed quota this week." She grasped at the lowest limb and hauled herself up in perfect tomboy fashion. "Do you know what I did this week, cat? I advertised for a delivery boy, and then I hired three little old ladies instead. Now they're doing the baking, and I'm doing the delivering." Berry stopped to catch her breath. "I'm not a delivery sort of person. I get lost a lot, and I'm not too brave about knocking on strange doors. And if that isn't bad enough . . . I moved the old ladies into my apartment." The kitten looked at her and blinked. Berry sighed in exasperation. "Well, what could I do? They were living in the train station."

Berry wriggled next to the kitten and tipped her head towards the stars. It was nice in the tree. The wind whistled through the limbs and whipped her short hair around her face. People should sit in trees more often, she decided. It was peaceful and exciting, all at the same time. And you could see forever, practically, clear down to the little bridge at the lower end of Ellenburg Drive. She watched in quiet fascination as headlights smoothly moved over the bridge and snaked uphill towards her. The soft rumble of an expensive car broke the silence. "Oh, lord," she breathed, suddenly aware of her predicament, "Large Pizza with the Works is coming home, and I'm sitting in his tree!"

Berry stared openmouthed as a *Great Gatsby*-type car purred up the driveway. It was a large, cream-colored machine with a brown leather convertible top, spoked wheels, and running boards. A Stutz Bearcat, she thought. Or maybe a Stanley Steamer. Definitely something old and flashy, and perfectly restored. The garage doors automatically opened, swallowed up the antique car, and closed with a neat click, plunging Berry and the cat back into quiet darkness.

Berry exhaled a low whistle. "Impressive," she told the cat. "This guy has style and money. Probably some eccentric gangster. Some drug runner who's watched too many old movies." She imagined him as looking like Quasimodo in a panama hat. The white pizza box caught her attention. She should probably deliver it, she sighed guiltily. Quasimodo was home now and might be hungry. After all, she did take pride in her job. Neither rain, nor sleet, nor snow shall keep her from delivering pizza. Of course there was nothing in that zippy little slogan about weird people and spooky houses. Maybe what she'd do is leave the box on the porch, ring the bell, and run like hell. She tucked the kitten under her arm and slithered closer to the tree trunk. There didn't seem to be any branches within stepping range. "Don't worry, cat," she mumbled. "If I got up . . ."

While she considered her next move a hall light sparkled at the other side of the house, and then a light flashed on directly in front of her. It was a bedroom. Quasi's bedroom. And she was sitting eye level to it, getting a crystal-clear picture of one of the most mouth-watering males she'd ever seen—over six feet tall with broad shoulders and slim hips and wavy almost-black hair that curled over his ears and scraped his crisp white shirt collar. Definitely not Quasimodo.

He flung a book onto the bed and popped the top button of his shirt open. Then another button. Then another. Berry involuntarily inched closer to the window. If he was a gangster she should be able to give the FBI a detailed description. She should watch closely and check for hidden weapons and identifying scars. He pulled the shirt off and draped it over a chair. Berry closed her eyes for a split second and swallowed. Definitely no hunchback. Just lots of muscle in all the right places, and a flat stomach with a silken line of black hair twirling around his navel, leading to his . . . Holy cow! He was unzipping his pants.

Berry felt her face flame. "I've got to get down," she whispered to the cat. "I've got to get out of here." Berry desperately looked for a foothold, willing her eyes to behave themselves and not return to the window. This wasn't the sort of thing pizza delivery ladies were supposed to do. Peeping in men's bedroom windows was a definite no-no. It was rude and immoral and could get you into a whole bunch of trouble. In fact, there was something about this man that smacked of trouble, Berry decided. It was his ability to fascinate, to mesmerize, to incite riot in a woman's body . . . in *her* body. Her body hadn't rioted in a long time. Working fourteen hours a day making pizzas didn't leave much time or energy for romance. Lately, she'd been convinced her hormones were in premature retirement, but there was something about this man that caught their attention. He was nice to watch. He moved with the fluid efficiency of an athlete, and there was something else . . . something more elusive than appreciation of healthy muscle. There was a good-humored set to his mouth, and a roguish imperiousness to his dark eyes.

Berry instinctively knew that, with or without clothes, the man was a menace to mental health and glandular stability. And she was dying to take one more peek. Before she even knew what her wide blue eyes had done, they had focused on Mr. Trouble. He was stripped to a pair of navy bikini briefs. He stuck his thumbs into the elastic waistband, gave a downward tug, and . . .

"Holy cow!" Berry gasped, covering her face with her hands. Her heart jumped to her throat as she lost her balance, and went flying. Her leg scraped against a lower limb as it cracked under her falling weight. She frantically grasped for branches as she fell, and then WUMP! She landed flat on her back, knocking the air out of her lungs. She lay perfectly still while little black dots floated in front of her eyes and the ocean pounded in her ears.

A few seconds—or was it hours—later, Berry blinked at the hunk of masculinity that bent over her. "Am I dead?"

"Not yet."

"I feel dead. I must be bleeding. My back is all warm and sticky."

He squatted beside her and looked more closely. "I don't see any blood, just some pizza sauce oozing through this crumpled box. Lady, you've squished this poor pizza to smithereens." He extracted the pizza box. "Is this mine?"

Berry nodded. She was relieved to find that he was fully clothed in a pair of jeans and a navy hooded sweatshirt. She made an attempt to sit up and began a methodical check of any bones that might be broken.

"What happened? I heard something crashing around out here, and there you were . . . lying on my pizza. Are you okay?" He picked bits of bark from her tangled hair. He glanced at the profusion of broken branches scattered on the ground and understanding flickered behind observant eyes. His attention turned to the tree, traveling up the height of it, resting on the large limb just outside his bedroom window. Incredulity registered on his face. "Lady, you must be kidding! You can't be that hard up to see a naked man."

Berry blushed clear to the roots of her hair. "I'm not hard up at all. I've seen lots of naked men."

He raised his eyebrows. "Lots?"

Berry stood up and tried to dust off the seat of her jeans. "Well, maybe not lots. A few. Actually, not too many." She threw her hands into the air in frustration. "Well, dammit, I've been busy. I don't have time to go around looking at naked men. I have a pizza business to run. I have old ladies to take care of. And anyway, you've got this all wrong. I was rescuing a kitten."

They both looked up at the tree. No kitten.

Berry pointed. "There was a kitten up there!"

"Uh-huh."

The hunk didn't believe her! Of all the nerve. Berry tipped her nose up and gave him her most withering look. Well, phooey on you, her most withering look said. I don't care what you think, anyway. She retrieved the pizza box and thrust it into his hands. "Here, this is yours. Twelve ninety-five, please."

His mouth dropped open.

Berry felt another blush coming on. That probably was a little high for a smashed pizza. "Well, hell," she amended, "the darn thing is free."

He watched in dismay as tomato sauce oozed over the sides of the box, onto his fingers. "Yuck."

Berry hesitated for a moment, intrigued by his

mouth. It sort of turned up at the corners. It was probably the greatest mouth she'd ever seen.

"Are you going to kiss me?"

Berry snapped to attention. "Certainly not!"

Laugh lines crinkled around mercurial eyes. "You were staring at my mouth."

"It's a terrific mouth."

He chuckled softly, and Berry watched in flustered annoyance as he considered her tangled blond curls and large cornflower-blue eyes. His inspection moved to her red down vest, plaid shirt and faded jeans. "I suppose you're the owner of that delapidated jeep."

"That jeep is not delapidated. That jeep is almost in A-One condition."

As if on cue, there was a loud *spronnnng* at curbside, and the jeep slowly began rolling backwards, down Ellenburg Drive. They both stood like statues, rooted to the spot in horror for several seconds before responding to the emergency.

"My jeep!" Berry finally exclaimed, sprinting across the lawn after the escaping vehicle. The jeep picked up speed on a downhill curve, jumped the curb, merrily bounced over a grassy area and headed for an opening between two large birch trees. Berry raced alongside the runaway car and reached for the door handle. Her fingers had just touched metal when she was tackled from behind and thrown to the ground. She picked her head up in time to see the jeep squeeze between the two trees and catapult itself off a twenty-foot cliff.

"Get off!" she gasped, twisting under her assailant. "You must weigh two hundred pounds."

"One seventy-eight and it's all muscle."

Berry already knew the part about it being all magnificent muscle. Besides being permanently engraved in her brain, she could feel it being firmly pressed into her flesh. They were lying zipper to zipper, his knee cozily nudging against the inside of her leg, his chest skimming against her breasts as he rested on his elbows, his delicious mouth hovering just inches above her own. Berry felt her stomach tumble and a flash of heat scorched her abdomen and headed south. She blinked at the tingling behind her nipples, unable to believe the effect this man was having on her quickly overheating body. She was in lust. No doubt about it.

A small smile tugged at his mouth while his eyes darkened. "You're staring at my mouth, again," he murmured in a voice that reminded Berry of fine smoky whiskey and clingy satin teddies.

Berry felt her mouth open, but no sound emerged. She unconsciously licked her lips and wondered if he could feel her heart pounding under her flannel shirt. He was going to kiss her. She could see it in his eyes and in the softening of his mouth. She could feel it in the way his body suddenly relaxed into hers. She splayed her hands against his shoulders to push him away—then watched in fascinated horror as her brain sent erroneous messages to her fingers, causing them to curl into his shirt and pull him closer.

His lips brushed against hers tentatively. It was a hello kiss, soft, warm, and undemanding. They watched each other for a moment with wary eyes, astonished at the intensity of the attraction, assessing the foolishness of their actions. Berry wondered at the emotions flickering across his face. Surprise. Resignation? Definitely determination as he suddenly claimed her mouth in a kiss that was fiercely possessive and blatantly hungry.

His tongue surged over hers, probing, tasting, testing her response, causing a thrill to race along her spine while panic rocketed in her brain. She'd started out to deliver a pizza, and now she as lying under a hundred and seventy-eight pounds of throbbing virility, getting her socks kissed off—and who knows what other pieces of clothing would follow! The panic turned to anger at herself, at him, at the dumb cat that lured her into his tree, at her jeep for irresponsibly committing suicide.

He broke from the kiss and eyed her speculatively. "I have the feeling your mind isn't on this kiss."

Berry wriggled free and stood on shaking legs. "Darn right it isn't." She gestured vigorously. "That was my jeep. I needed it. I can't deliver pizzas without it. You had no business jumping on me like that."

"Are you crazy? You would have killed yourself."

"Well, fine. Now I'll slowly die of starvation because I'm deprived of earning a living." She turned on her heel and strode off to the birch trees to inspect the damage. Of all the rotten luck, she fumed. She'd gotten that jeep two years ago, the day after her divorce had been finalized, and it had never given her a moment's trouble. Of course, she had to give it a quart of oil every Friday. And it did look a little disreputable with all that rust and the coat hanger antenna, but those things were cosmetic. Not everyone could afford a fancy car like Hot Stuff here.

They stood at the edge of the cliff and gazed down at the jeep, belly-up and slightly squashed in the moonlight.

Berry sighed in morose resignation. "It's dead."

"Doesn't look good."

Berry pulled herself up to all of her five feet six inches and stuck her chin out. "Oh, well." It was all she could think to say. After all, what on earth can you say when your entire future has just gone over a cliff? What can you say when faced with certain bankruptcy? What can you say when you practically attacked a man and then changed your mind in midstream? And I'm not going to cry, she told herself, frowning. I absolutely am not going to cry.

He studied her face in the moonlight. "You're not going to cry, are you?"

"Absolutely not." A large tear oozed over her lower lashes and streaked down her cheek. "Damn."

He put an arm around her shoulders and wiped the tear away with his thumb. "It's not so bad. The insurance will pay to replace the jeep."

Berry tried to blink back another tear, and scolded herself for getting so emotional over a silly car. In all honesty, the thing was a hunk of junk. It's just that it was her hunk of junk. Her only hunk of junk, and it would take hundreds of pizzas to replace it.

"You don't have insurance," he sighed.

"Not that kind. Only if I run over somebody." She squared her shoulders and wiped away the last remnant of tears. "Well, good-bye."

He walked beside her. "Where are you going?"

"Home."

"That must be miles from here."

Berry shrugged. "It's not so far." May as well get used to walking, she thought, I'm going to be doing a lot of it. Anyway, she could use the exercise to get rid of the butterflies Navy Briefs was producing in her stomach. One sidelong glance from him had the same effect on her nervous system as seven cups of coffee . . . especially now that she knew how he kissed.

"If you'll wait a minute, I'll give you a ride."

"Thanks, but that's not necessary. Besides, I'd get your fancy car all dirty."

"My fancy car has leather seats. They wash. Wait here."

Berry kept walking. "Really, it's not—"

He grabbed her firmly by the shoulders and plunked her into a sitting position on the edge of the curb. *"Wait here!"*

"You're awfully bossy."

"So I've been told."

That intrigued her. She watched him jog away and wondered who else thought he was bossy. A girlfriend, maybe? A wife? She put her hand to her stomach. Thoughts of wives and girlfriends made her feel queasy.

She was still wondering when the cream-colored car rolled to a stop in front of her. She removed her vest and carefully placed it on the floor, mozzarella side up. "This is very nice of you."

He grinned at her and extended his hand. "Jake Sawyer, all-around nice guy."

Berry looked at the hand and shivered. She was sure if she touched it her hair would stand on end, or at the very least, she'd giggle, or stammer, or blush for the umpteenth time that night. She swallowed, steadied herself and took a firm grip. "Berry Knudsen."

"Berry? Like in holly berry or cranberry?"

"Lingonberry. My mother was inordinately proud of her Scandinavian heritage." She pulled her hand away and tucked it into her lap for safekeeping, feeling like a flustered teenager. She frantically searched for an innocuous topic for conversation and blurted out, "So, who else thinks you're bossy? Your wife?"

Jake Sawyer looked embarrassed. He mumbled something unintelligible, and Berry thought his face flushed slightly under a five o'clock shadow. That made her feel better. There was something incredibly comforting about Jake Sawyer's blushing. "Sorry," she murmured, "I didn't do that too smoothly."

Jake smiled. "You remind me of my kids. No guile. Whatever's on your mind just pops out."

His kids? He had kids. And a wife. And he'd just kissed her. She was going to go straight home and brush her teeth. "How many kids do you have?"

"Twenty-one. This morning they all told me the same thing you did. They think I'm bossy."

"Twenty-one kids?"

"I teach first grade. And to answer your first question, I'm not married."

Berry felt her mouth fall open and almost laughed with relief. He wasn't married. Not that it really mattered to her. She wasn't interested in men right now. She especially wasn't interested in this man. Still, it was good to know she hadn't kissed a philanderer. She hadn't spied on someone else's private property. She hadn't smashed a family pizza. And this tantalizing macho hulk, driving a megabucks car, taught first grade! "You don't look like a first-grade teacher."

"I know," he groaned. "I'm too big. I don't fit in any of the little chairs. My fingers aren't good at holding crayons or safety scissors. And I can't get the hang of barrettes at all." He slumped in his seat. "I wasn't cut out for first grade. This is the toughest thing I've ever done."

The image of Jake Sawyer playing mother hen to a group of seven-year-olds brought a smile to Berry's lips. If she'd had a first-grade teacher that looked like Jake Sawyer, she'd have done anything to stay after school. Her first-grade teacher had been five feet two inches tall and weighed close to two hundred pounds. Mrs. Berman. Berry shivered at the memory.

"Earth to Berry."

"Sorry. I guess I drifted off."

"I was afraid you might have sustained a head injury when you fell out of the tree."

"No. The only thing damaged is my pride and your pizza." She squinted into the darkness. "Turn right at the next light. Then just go straight until you see the sign, PIZZA PLACE."

"This isn't exactly a ritzy part of town."

Berry shrugged. "It's an ethnic neighborhood. Italian bakery. Vietnamese laundry. Ethiopian restaurant. Everybody's struggling to make a start, like me."

Jake executed a smooth corner at the light and frowned at the dark street lined with grimy stores and intersected by narrow alleyways. "Why have you chosen to work in this pizza place?"

"Why did you choose to teach first grade?"

Jake smiled wryly. "If I tell you, will you tell me?"

"I hope your story's more interesting than mine."

"I invented Gunk."

"Gunk?"

"It creeps. It crawls. It comes in five scents and three flavors. It's edible. It's freezable. It's disgusting."

"I've seen it advertised on tv."

"I invented it. I was working for Bartlow Labs, looking for an inexpensive organic glue, and I discovered Gunk."

"Are you a chemist?"

"I used to be. I quit the second I sold my Gunk rights. I hated the fluorescent lights and the nine-to-five routine. And it was boring. Glue is boring." He smiled proudly. "Now I'm an inventor."

"What about teaching first grade?"

"Guinea pigs. I have twenty-one kids to test my new ideas. Besides, I had a teaching degree and I needed the money. I squandered my Gunk money on this car and that monstrous Victorian house."

Berry wrinkled her nose. The man had forsaken a respectable profession to invent future Gunk, and thought of seven-year-olds as guinea pigs. Prince Charming had some frog in him. "How did you ever get the school board to hire you?"

"Luckily, Mrs. Newfarmer had a nervous breakdown and suddenly abandoned her first-grade class. When I applied for a job as substitute teacher, they were desperate enough to consider me."

"Nervous breakdown? Must be some group of kids."

"The kids are terrific. Mrs. Newfarmer had martial problems."

Hmmm, she thought, I can relate to that. Marriage could easily give somebody a nervous breakdown. It could give you hives, and dishpan hands and paranoia. She should know. She'd tried it. Four years of struggling to put her husband through medical school, and then she'd found him playing doctor with Mary Lou Marowski. Yes sir, she knew all about marriage.

"Well? What about you? Why are you working in this . . . ethnic neighborhood?"

"I was married while still in college. We couldn't both afford to go to school full time, so I quit and went to work. When my marriage fell apart after four years I didn't think I could manage a job that required much mental concentration or emotional energy. I wanted something to do with my hands. Something that was physically exhausting. And I wanted something that was close to the university so I could return to school part time. Well, here it is. The Pizza Place. I worked as a pizza maker for a year, and when the owner retired seven months ago, I scraped together every cent I could find, mortgaged my soul, and bought the business."

Jake parked at the curb and considered the two-story yellow brick building. A gaudy red neon sign flashed out PIZZA PLACE in the ground-floor picture window. White ruffled curtains hung in the four second-story windows. "You live upstairs?"

"Yup."

"Alone?"

"Not anymore. I adopted three old ladies this week."

Jake raised his eyebrows.

"It's a long story." Berry eased herself out of the car, relieved to put some distance between her and Jake Sawyer. The man was physically disturbing. He gave her hot flashes. She wasn't even sure if she liked him. He bought extravagant cars and eccentric houses. He thumbed his nose at security. The man was a risk-taker with big dreams.

Berry had small dreams. She wanted a college education. She wanted a window that overlooked a meadow, or a creek, or a green lawn bordered by flower beds. She wanted a nice boring husband who believed in monogamy, but she didn't want him now. First the college education, then the husband, then the lawn. That was the plan. It certainly didn't include falling head over teakettles for awesome Jake Sawyer. And the worst part about all this was that she'd acted so dopey! She'd fallen out of his tree onto a pizza. Good lord.

Berry's back ached, her arms were scratched, and her jeans had a large hole in the knee. She mumbled an embarrassed thank you, carefully closed the door of Jake's expensive car, and beat a hasty retreat to her apartment. Not one of her better days. She'd peeked in Jake Sawyer's bedroom window and ogled his body, and now she was being punished. How else could you explain the jeep suicide? Berry trudged up the narrow stairs. At least the score should be even now. Her jeep for thirty seconds of Jake Sawyer practically nude—seemed like a fair price.

Berry gnawed at her lower lip. How was she ever going to replace the stupid jeep. She didn't have a dime in the bank, and she had nowhere to go for credit. What a rotten break. Just when she was making some progress. Last week she'd gotten two lunch contracts at local businesses. How was she going to deliver pizzas without the jeep? "Damn," she said, trudging up the narrow stairs. "Double damn."

Mrs. Dugan stood ramrod-straight with righteous indignation at the head of the stairs. "Hmmm, fine talk for a young lady. I may as well tell you right now, I don't tolerate cussing."

A second grey-haired lady appeared in the doorway. "For goodness sakes, Sara, all she said was damn. Damn doesn't hardly count as a cussword. Young people say things like that nowadays."

A third voice chimned in, "You're right, Mildred, what should she say? Oh, fudge? Darn? It's not the same, not the same at all. Sometimes you need to let loose with a good cuss. In fact, I feel like cussing right now." The plump old lady uttered an expletive that made double damn sound like polite conversation and raised everyone's eyebrows, including Berry's.

"Mrs. Fitz!"

Mrs. Fitz slapped her leg and chuckled. "That was a beauty, wasn't it? See, I feel much better now."

Berry wearily walked across the room and sank into the Boston rocker.

"Good heavens," Mrs. Fitz exclaimed, "what happened to you? You're a mess."

Berry sniffed back a tear. "I fell out of a tree onto the large pizza with the works . . . and then the jeep drove itself over a cliff."

Mrs. Dugan set a bowl of soapy water at Berry's feet and began gently dabbing at her scratched cheek. "You aren't hurt serious, are you? You have anything worse than these scratches and scrapes?"

"Nope. I'm okay." Berry smiled. It had been a long time since she'd had this sort of motherly attention. Her own mother was miles away in McMinneville, Oregon, and Allen, her ex-husband, had never given her much attention. She was still amazed at how marriage could be such a lonely way of life. Four years of living with a man who never remembered her birthday or noticed a wayward tear. She'd been so impressed with his cool intelligence and professional aspirations that she'd jumped into marriage without considering his emotional limitations. Thank goodness all that was behind her. She was older and wiser and pleased with her hard-won independence.

"Hello," Jake Sawyer called from the top of the stairs.

"Goodness," Mrs. Fitz exclaimed, "who's the hunk?"

"I'm Berry's friend."

Mrs. Dugan gaped at him in dumbfounded silence, her hand frozen in midair.

Jake noticed the water and blood dripping from Berry's arm and gently removed the wet cloth from Mrs. Dugan's fingers. He soaked the cloth and applied it to Berry's scratches.

Berry stiffened at his gentle touch. Having Mrs. Dugan swab away the dirt and blood was one thing. Having Jake Sawyer minister to her wounds was disturbingly intimate. Beyond intimate. It was tender and caring and absolutely unwanted. She clenched her teeth, narrowed her eyes, and hoped she looked menacing. "What are you doing here?"

"Damned if I know. I was sitting down there at

the curb and couldn't get myself to drive off. I kept getting this mental picture of you standing out on the highway, thumbing a ride with a pizza box stuck under your arm."

"So?"

"So I didn't like it." His dark eyes searched hers. "You're really in a bind, aren't you?"

"I'll figure something out."

Jake's mouth quirked into an embarrassed grin. "I have a confession to make. That was my cat in the tree. She gets up there all the time."

Berry's eyes opened wide. "You acted like I was a Peeping Tom."

"Well? Were you peeping?"

"Only a little!" She felt her blood pressure rise. It wasn't her fault. She had been in that tree doing a good deed, and he'd practically flaunted himself at her. She sprang out of the chair and stood with her fists on her hips. "It was unavoidable. You got undressed right in front of the window. Don't you believe in shades? What are you, some kind of exhibitionist?"

"I just moved in. I haven't had time to put shades up. Anyway, there aren't any neighbors for miles."

Berry turned on her heel and glared at the three ladies who were "tsking" behind her. She frowned and wrinkled her nose in a look that said, *One word out of any of you and it's back to the train station.*

Jake held his hands up. "Wait. I didn't come up here to discuss your voyeuristic tendencies—"

"Voyeuristics tendencies! Of all the . . . you are the most . . . I am not!" Berry closed her eyes and took several deep breaths. She opened her eyes and made a flamboyant gesture with her arm, pointing to the door. "Out!"

Jake took a seat in the vacant rocking chair

and accepted a cup of cocoa from Mrs. Fitz. "Boy, she sure can get riled."

"Yeah, ain't she a pip?"

Berry spun around and flapped her arms at Mrs. Fitz. "Mrs. Fitz, anyone can see this man is leaving. We don't serve cocoa to men who are leaving."

"Nonsense. He's all settled in here." Mrs. Fitz pressed her lips together in satisfaction. "Don't he look nice and comfy."

Mildred brought him a plate of chocolate chip cookies. "We just baked these fresh tonight." She turned to Mrs. Fitz. "Goodness, it's nice to have a man in the house."

"Makes me want to put on some fresh lipstick" Mrs. Fitz laughed. "Too bad I haven't got any."

Mildred put her arm around plump little Mrs. Fitz. "That's okay. Pretty soon you'll have money to buy some lipstick."

"Berry's hired us," Mrs. Fitz explained to Jake. "We were just about scraping by on our social security checks, living in the Southside Hotel for Ladies, and then they decided to renovate the building and turn it into fancy condominiums. We couldn't afford anyplace else. We looked real hard, but there just wasn't a room cheap enough. Finally, they evicted us. We were temporarily holed up in the train station when we saw Berry's ad in the paper." Mrs. Fitz grinned. She was five feet tall with short steel-gray hair that had been permed into two inches of frizz. She was apple-cheeked with an ample chest and dimples in her elbows and stout knees. "We know we're a bunch of old ladies, but we figured the three of us together might be able to hold down a job. Sort of a package deal."

Mildred pulled a kitchen chair close to the rocker. "We walked all over town for days trying to get a job and then Berry hired us. We'd just about given up."

"This business with the jeep isn't gonna change things, is it?" Mrs. Fitz worried. "How bad is the jeep?"

"All the king's horses and all the king's men can't put the jeep back together again," Berry told her.

Jake downed the last of the cocoa and stood to leave. "It's okay, Mrs. Fitz. Berry's going to use my car till she can replace the jeep."

Berry looked at him wide-eyed. "I can't deliver pizzas in your car."

Jake somberly chewed a cookie. "It was my cat that started this fiasco. I feel responsible." He leaned close to Berry and whispered in an aside, "Besides, you're one heck of a kisser."

Berry ignored the heat that burned in her cheeks. "I can't deliver pizzas in a forty-thousand-dollar car!"

Mrs. Fitz whistled behind her. "You mean he looks like this, and he's rich too?"

"I invented Gunk."

Mrs. Fitz's eyes popped wide open. "That disgusting slimy stuff you can eat? I love that stuff."

Jake turned to Berry. She was sure he would kiss her, but he tweaked her hair instead. "My school is just three blocks from here. I'll drop the car off on my way to work tomorrow morning."

Two

Berry looked at the stacks of pizza boxes and wondered how she was ever going to get them all into Jake Sawyer's two-seater. Eighteen large pizzas and seven small, all due at Windmere Technicals by twelve-thirty. She groaned. If it hadn't been for these lunch contracts she would never have accepted Jake's offer. The car was too expensive, too powerful, too exotic. What if she scratched it? The car was perfect, for crying out loud. How could anything that old look so new? We aren't talking about a two-hundred-dollar jeep here. We're talking about an outrageously extravagant toy in mint condition.

And what about Jake Sawyer? Another toy in mint condition who was too powerful, too expensive, and too exotic. She'd spent half the night reviewing his kiss and knew she didn't want it repeated. It wasn't the sort of kiss that could be easily forgotten. It was the sort of kiss that could make you lose perspective, lose sight of important goals. She'd interrupted her education once for a man, and she wasn't about to make the same mistake again. She would borrow Jake's car only until she could find a better solution to her problem, and she would put as much distance as she could between herself and its owner.

She speared the car keys with her pinky finger and pushed through the front door, balancing six large pizza boxes in her outstretched arms. She squinted into the light drizzle, wondering where Jake had parked. He'd said the car was directly in front of the Pizza Place. Berry held the door open with her foot. "Mrs. Fitz, you took the keys from Jake this morning. Where'd he park the car?"

Mrs. Fitz wiped her chubby hands on her big white apron and shook her head. "Goodness sakes, child, the car's right in front of you. It's right here in front of the . . ." Mrs. Fitz's little round mouth dropped open. "Where's the car?"

"Maybe Jake moved it. Maybe he changed his mind and—"

"I don't think so. We've got his keys."

Berry felt the blood drain from her face. "Oh, no, the car's gone. How could this happen?"

"Looks to me like it's been stolen."

Berry staggered back into the store and deposited the pizza boxes on the counter. Jake Sawyer's car had been stolen. She'd had possession of it exactly three and a half hours, and it now had gotten itself stolen. A slow dull throb began in her temples.

"Jake's not gonna be happy about this," Mrs. Fitz whispered.

"Maybe I'll join a convent, or move to Rio."

Mrs. Fitz dialed a number. "I'm calling a taxi to deliver the pizzas. You stay here and call the police. Maybe they'll get the car back before Jake gets out of school."

Berry's face brightened. That was a hopeful thought. It wasn't exactly a run-of-the-mill auto.

The police would probably have an easy time finding it.

Four hours later, Mrs. Fitz placed a plate of cookies and a glass of milk in front of Jake. "It's not so bad. Nobody's been hurt. You just lost your car for awhile."

Jake stared glassy-eyed at the cookies, and Berry thought he looked like a man who'd just been told aliens had landed in the Safeway parking lot.

Mrs. Dugan patted his hand. "We filed a police report. The officers said they'd be sure to find an odd car like that."

"It's unique. I had it specially restored. There's not another one like it in the whole world."

Big deal, Berry fumed as she pounded pizza dough on the large wooden counter behind Jake. It wasn't right that the car had been stolen, and she really did feel sorry for Jake, but why on earth would anyone want such a car? Double-barreled chrome widgets and an engine that could pull a freight train. The leather upholstery on the darn thing probably cost more than her yearly income.

Berry slapped a wad of dough onto the floured surface and wondered why she was so mad. If Jake Sawyer wanted such a flashy car, so what? No skin off her nose if he had to enhance his ego with a piece of machinery that was obviously designed to augment a certain male body part. She paused in her silent ranting and raving to admit that his ego really didn't seem to need enhancing. And from what she'd seen in the tree, the rest of him didn't need any augmenting either.

So what was she mad about, anyway? Maybe it was the way he'd perched on a stool and calmly listened to all of the theft details in a trancelike state, occasionally muttering phrases like, "I knew I was doomed the minute I laid eyes on her." What the devil was that supposed to mean? Berry flattened the dough into a round circle. She suspected he thought she was a walking disaster.

Mrs. Fitz peered across the counter at Berry. "Good heavens, child, you're just about beating that poor dough to death."

Berry sighed. For a full year after her divorce she'd taken her frustrations out on pizza dough. If it hadn't been for pizza dough she might have turned into a homicidal maniac. Then little by little her life had fallen into place, her sunny disposition had returned, peace and purpose had replaced the disorder of disillusionment.

Berry poked at the massacred dough. She'd known Jake Sawyer for less than twenty-four hours and here she was smashing innocent pizza dough again. The man was a threat to her sanity. He gave her an upset stomach. He made her act like a boob, blushing and stammering and falling out of trees.

She paused for more sober, honest introspection and admitted that the real source of her anger was much more complex. Jake Sawyer made her hungry. She wanted to watch him move, talk to him, touch him. It was as if she'd straggled through a desert and suddenly come upon a chocolate ice cream soda. It wasn't fair that such a forbidden treat should be dangled in front of her. Chocolate sodas gave her hives, and Berry was certain that if she gave Jake Sawyer half a chance he could produce hives too. He could also produce heartache, insecurity and the gnawing loneliness of unrequited love.

I don't need this, Berry thought with a scowl, taking a swipe at the dough with her wooden rolling pin. Someday I'll be ready for another relationship—but not now. First, I get the Pizza Place on its feet. Second, I get my degree. Third . . .

Third was interrupted by the phone ringing.

Mrs. Fitz answered and smiled, her round cheeks looking like polished apples. "It's the police. They've found the car!"

Jake stared at the address Mrs. Fitz had written. "The corner of Grande and Seventeenth Street."

Berry pulled her vest over a gray hooded sweatshirt. "I know where that is. It's less than half a mile from here. We can walk."

Jake stood in the doorway, zipped his parka and took a grim assessment of the neighborhood. A cold mist drizzled down the grimy brick facades of nearby stores, and intermittent gusts of wind buffeted plate-glass windows. Sodden newspapers and assorted litter slapped against doorways and clogged gutters. A mongrel slunk with his tail between his legs on the opposite side of the street.

Berry knew what Jake was seeing. He was seeing bars at first-floor windows installed to prevent burglaries. He was seeing the empty beer cans and wine bottles that hadn't made it into trash cans. He was imagining thugs lurking in the alleys and poverty hiding behind closed doors. She felt the need to defend her home. "It's not all that bad," Berry offered. "You see that cheery yellow light in the window above Giovanni's Grocery? That's Mrs. Giovanni making supper. In the summer she hangs window boxes from her kitchen window and fills them with red geraniums. The apartment building next to me houses four generations of Lings. Last year Charlie Ling won first prize at his school science fair. And down the street—"

Jake grinned and ruffled her hair. "You're kind of cute when you get territorial. So you really like this neighborhood?"

Berry shrugged. "It's okay. I'd rather look out my window and see a meadow or a mountain, but instead I have Mrs. Giovanni's bold red geraniums. I try to make the best of it."

He was silent for a moment. Berry thought she caught a glimmer of gruding admiration and was horrified at the amount of pleasure it produced. She turned her embarrassingly radiant face into the wind, away from Jake's scrutiny. "This way," she mumbled, heading for Grande.

Jake snagged her by the arms. "Hold it, Goldilocks, where's your umbrella?"

"I don't own an umbrella."

"Then at least put your hood up."

"I hate wearing hoods."

"Mrs. Dugan would take her wooden spoon to you if she caught you out in the rain like this without a hat," he whispered conspiratorily.

"I'm twenty-six years old, and I don't need Mrs. Dugan—"

Jake Sawyer grinned and kissed her on the tip of her wet nose and then on her slightly parted lips. It wasn't a kiss that said *I love you,* or *Let's go to bed.* It was a kiss that said *Shut up, you adorable goose.*

The kiss traveled through Berry's body like heated honey, diffusing her outrage. She wasn't at all happy about being an adorable goose, but the kiss had felt terrific. As much as she hated to admit it, she thoroughly enjoyed kissing Jake Sawyer. In fact, she had half a mind to return his kiss with interest.

"I'm not even going to guess what's going through your mind. You're looking at me as if I were lunch."

"I am not. That's ridiculous." What a rat. Now he could read minds.

Sawyer tipped his head back and laughed. It was a full, rich laugh that was impossible to ignore. A devilish look came into his eyes, and he

moved closer, pressing Berry against the door-
jamb. He brushed his lips against hers as he spoke.
"What I need is another kiss . . . to help me forget
about my car."

"No!"

"Don't you like kissing men?"

"I don't have time to go around kissing men."

"You only have time to climb trees and watch
them undress?"

"Yes. No!"

"I have to admit, it's a little arousing knowing
that you've seen me naked."

"I didn't see you naked. I fell out of the tree
before you got to the really good stuff." Actually,
his blue briefs had been quite revealing. She felt
her face flame and knew Jake Sawyer was enjoying her discomfort.

"Shame on you," he grinned. "I think you're
telling fibs."

"Good grief."

He pulled her hood over her head and tied the
drawstring securely into a bow, making her feel
five years old. Without saying another word he
took her hand and pulled her along beside him.

As they approached Grande Street Berry felt his
grip tighten. Big, strong Jake Sawyer was nervous. He really did like his silly car. Berry didn't
know much about cars, but she knew about losing things you love. She knew about the pain and
anxiety such a loss produced. A rush of compas-
sion swept through Berry, creating an overwhelming urge to rush out and buy Jake Sawyer a gallon
of his favorite ice cream. Berry squeezed his hand
and sent him her most comforting smile.

Jake seemed surprised at the gesture. He glanced
down at her and allowed his feelings to surface.
"I'm kind of nervous."

"I guessed."

"Probably it's okay."

"Probably." With the way my luck's been running, Berry thought, that car'll be picked cleaner than a turkey carcass the day after Thanksgiving.

They turned the corner and found several officers standing hands on hips by a black-and-white squad car, inspecting an article at curbside. It took several seconds before Jake and Berry recognized the object of their curiosity. At first glance it seemed to be a piece of scrap metal resting on four cinder blocks.

Jake expelled a well-chosen expletive that caused the officers to turn in his direction. "Is that my car?"

An elderly officer shook his head sadly. "Are you Jake Sawyer?"

Jake stretched his hands out in despair. "Oh, man! Look at this. There's nothing left. How could this happen so fast?"

"Modern technology."

Jake kicked at the cinder block and groaned.

Berry trotted beside him as he paced back and forth the length of the car. "It's not so bad. The insurance will buy you a new one. You do have insurance, don't you?"

"Of course I have insurance. Who cares about insurance. This car is irreplaceable."

"Nonsense. There must be plans somewhere. Just go back and get another."

"Get another? Berry, this isn't a fruitcake we're talking about. This was an exquisitely tuned, hand-crafted piece of machinery." Jake stopped pacing and plunged his hands into his pockets. "Anyway, this was my Gunk car. It was special," he added quietly.

Berry was beginning to understand. He'd given himself a present—not just a car, but a new life. No more fluorescent lights. No more boring glue.

Maybe squandering all his money on a house and a car was an act of confidence. Maybe it was like saying, *It's okay to spend all the Gunk money, because I'm going to be a success at my new career. I'm going to make a lot more money.* And now he'd lost his Gunk car, and maybe he was a little afraid he'd never be able to replace it.

Jake turned to the officer. "Do you know who did this?"

"We'll ask around. Sometimes we get lucky and come up with a name."

Jake stared morosely at his car. "This is damn depressing."

Berry tried to lighten the mood. She linked her arm through his and narrowed her eyes in mock annoyance. "This will never do, Sawyer," she scolded. "You're an inventor. You're supposed to be happy."

"Yeah, but this sad hunk of junk was my toy."

"Don't you have any other toys?"

He shook his head. "I'm really a very dull person. Work, work, work."

"That was back in your glue days. Now you're an inventor. Now it's play, play, play."

Berry was relieved to see the beginnings of a smile creep around the corners of his mouth, but she wasn't sure how she felt about the musing, slightly smoldering look that stole into his eyes. There was something very serious about that look. Something frightening and exciting.

Berry opened one eye and grimaced. Six o'clock in the morning and Mrs. Fitz was making tea. "Mrs. Fitz, don't you ever sleep?"

"Old people don't need so much sleep. Anyway, it isn't any fun sleeping with those two. They snore." Mrs. Fitz added a dollop of honey to her tea.

"Now, if I had a man in my bed . . . well, that'd be something different."

Berry straightened her flannel nightie and swung her legs over the side of the couch. The large front room of her apartment served as living room, dining room, and efficiency kitchen. The other smaller room, her bedroom, had been turned into a dormitory for the ladies. She liked the ladies and enjoyed their company, but she dearly missed the comfort of her nice, big bed. She rubbed a sore spot on her back and slid her feet into a pair of slippers that looked like raccoons.

"Maybe you should remarry." Berry yawned. "Have you ever thought about finding a husband?"

"I've been looking around, but I haven't seen anything I like yet. Now if I was younger I'd go for that Jake Sawyer. What a hunk."

Berry plugged the coffee pot in and sighed. Jake Sawyer was a hunk, all right. A hunk of trouble. She had an economics quiz later this morning that she'd totally forgotten about. Twenty-four hours of Jake Sawyer and already she was neglecting her studies. She opened the refrigerator and rattled a bunch of jars around.

"What are you looking for?" Mrs. Fitz asked.

"My coffee mug."

"Lordy, child, you aren't going to find it in there."

"Oh, yeah." Damn, she thought, this is what a sleepless night does to you. How could anyone get to sleep with visions of Jake Sawyer dancing in her head. Jake Sawyer in his one-of-a-kind car. Jake Sawyer in her kitchen. Jake Sawyer in his underwear. She filled her coffee mug with prune juice.

Mrs. Fitz raised her eyebrows. "I hope you're planning on staying close to home today. That's a lot of prune juice."

Berry peered into her mug and wrinkled her now. "Ugh. What is this?"

Mrs. Fitz rolled her eyes, dumped the juice down the drain and rinsed out Berry's mug. She filled the mug with coffee and handed it to Berry. "When you fell out of that tree, did you land on your head?"

"No. I landed on my pizza."

Mrs. Fitz looked at her shrewdly. "You're kind of stuck on that Sawyer guy."

"Yeah. Isn't that the pits."

Mrs. Fitz looked disgusted. "What a ninny."

Mrs. Dugan padded into the kitchen area. "Who's a ninny?"

"Lingonberry, here. She thinks love's a waste of time."

"Humph. Sometimes it is. Remember William Criswald? The old coot. I fancied that man for seven years and just when I was about to reel him in, he died. You can't count on men over seventy-five. You never know how long they're gonna last."

"Well, she isn't in love with an old goat like Criswald. She's in love with Jake Sawyer."

Berry smacked her coffee mug down on the counter, slopping hot coffee over her hand. "Ow! Dammit. I'm not in love with Jake Sawyer."

Mrs. Dugan and Mrs. Fitz exchanged glances and smiled slyly.

"I'm attracted to him, and I like him . . . usually."

Mrs. Fitz folded her sausage arms across ample breasts. "She's in love with him, all right," she whispered to Mrs. Dugan.

Berry took a cautious sip of coffee and gathered her books together. "I can't be in love with some-one I've only known for twenty-four hours."

"What about love at first sight?"

"It's rubbish. And besides, I refuse to be in love. I have other priorities, like taking an economics test that I'm totally unprepared for." She glanced at her watch and winced. She had no car, and she was late. "I have to run. I want to go to the library and try to get some studying in before my exam. Send the lunch contracts out by taxi again. I'll be back at three-thirty. Can you guys handle things?"

"Piece of cake."

Berry bolted down the stairs, only to be called back by Mrs. Fitz. "Lingonberry," she shouted, "you're gonna look awful silly going to class in them raccoon slippers and your nightgown."

Berry crossed her fingers as she skipped down the stairs ten minutes later. Please God, no more disasters. She closed the door behind her and took a deep breath of cold crisp air. The rain had stopped during the night, and the neighborhood looked freshly washed and waiting for spring. Berry grinned with the sheer joy of being alive and did a little jig as she watched her reflection in the TLC Cleaners plate-glass window.

She walked quickly and two blocks later she found herself approaching The Willard Street Elementary School. Jake's school. She smiled at the old two-story, red brick building. It brought back memories of her own school days in McMinneville, when each morning she would set off along quiet tree-lined streets with her little sister, Katie.

It was a childhood of few surprises. Tuna fish or peanut butter and jelly in your lunchbox. Hot oatmeal in the morning, homemade butterscotch pudding in the afternoon, and piano lessons every Thursday. For years, she and Katie wore sturdy red shoes with a wide strap and big silver buckle. Those red shoes represented the basic philosophy of the Knudsen household—middle of the road and casually practical. They were a compromise between shiny patent-leather Mary Janes and staunch brown oxfords.

Berry suddenly realized she'd been trying to reconstruct the stability of her childhood, with little success. Her mother had been a master of order and routine. Each mitten had its proper place, dinner was served promptly at five-thirty, the bathroom was always miraculously stocked with freshly laundered towels. It hadn't been a household of strict routine and unbending discipline. It had been a household of dull predictability and comfortable emotions.

And my life, Berry groaned, my life is chaos. The harder I try, the worse it gets. I wash the towels, but I never get around to folding them. I lose mittens before I can find a proper place for them, and dinner consists of staring into the refrigerator at six-thirty and wondering what the devil I can eat in a hurry. Now I have three old ladies living with me and my refrigerator is filled with prune juice and blood-pressure medicine. Berry shook her head at the Willard School. And to insure that my efforts at organization are a total loss, Jake Sawyer has appeared, destroying whatever emotional comfort I'd managed to reinstate into my life. Why? Why me?

Berry glanced at her watch and hurriedly moved on. She suspected she knew at least part of her problem. Days were too short. Twenty-four hours was simply not enough. If she had twenty-six she might have a chance to make butterscotch once in awhile.

Suddenly, the need to make butterscotch pudding was overwhelming. For six years she had postponed even the simplest pleasures while pursuing visions of success. Four years of that time had been spent insuring her husband's future. Now she was chasing after her own dreams. She was proud of her accomplishments, but she was starving for butterscotch pudding.

Tears burned the back of her eyes with the knowledge that there was no pudding in her immediate future. In fact, she would have to work twice as hard now that she had to replace the jeep.

She angrily scrubbed away a tear that had dribbled down her cheek, took a deep breath and reined in her emotions, admonishing herself that there was even less time in her life for self-pity than there was for pudding. She felt her sense of humor surface over the absurdity of her struggle, and laughingly promised herself that when she was done with college she would live on nothing but pudding.

Three

Berry saw the strange little puff of black smoke two and a half blocks away, but her mind was on other things—like her recent economics test and Jake Sawyer's smile. It wasn't until she turned the corner and saw the fire trucks that her mind contemplated disaster. Her heart skipped a beat and then felt as if it had stopped altogether. The trucks were in front of the Pizza Place. Fire hoses snaked across the sidewalk. Soot blackened the second-floor windows.

"No!" Berry shuddered, convulsively clapping her hand to her mouth. "Oh, Lord, no!" Mrs. Dugan, Mrs Fitz, and Mildred were supposed to be safely housed in that building. At this time of the afternoon they would be taking naps and making tea. They would be behind those four fire-blackened windows. Berry felt a scream lodge painfully in her throat. How could you grow to love three little old ladies so quickly? She'd known them less than a week, but they'd become a precious part of her life. She opened her mouth, but was too scared to cry. She blindly stumbled into the street and broke into a run. There were no thoughts in her mind, just fear and pain, throbbing in her stomach, pounding in her ears.

A hot flush of tears flooded her eyes when she caught sight of three curly white heads, bobbing behind a fire truck. Those grizzled, frizzy heads belonged to her ladies! They were safe! Berry felt dizzy with relief. She reached out with her hand to steady a wobbly world, feeling her knees crumple under her. She sank to the pavement and was engulfed in blackness that swirled and floated and roared through her brain.

Minutes later Berry struggled through the murk of semiconsciousness. She opened her eyes and smiled. "Thanks for the pudding, Mom."

Jake tightened his grip on her. "What?"

"The pudding. It was great."

"Honey, I'm not your mom. Look at me."

Berry blinked and concentrated, shaking the last of the cobwebs away. Did she just call Jake Sawyer Mom? He felt like Mom. Strong and reassuring, pressing kisses against her temple, into her hair. She could get used to this. This could be habit-forming. Jake Sawyer was going to make some woman a wonderful mother . . . except he looked awful. Grime streaked his face, emphasizing the grim set to his mouth and the cold fear in his red-rimmed eyes. Berry touched her fingertip to a sweat-soaked ringlet that had fallen across his forehead. "You look terrible."

Jake broke into a grin, his teeth seeming extraordinarily white in the soot-darkened face. "I'm okay. Are you okay?"

"Of course."

"You fainted."

"That's what happens to you when you don't make time for breakfast. You get wimpy. My mother warned me this would happen."

The stricken look had entirely left Jake's face. It was replaced with an only moderately successful attempt at anger. "Don't ever skip breakfast again. It's enough to scare the daylights out of someone."

Berry smiled in amazement. That frantic look to his eyes had been for her. He'd been worried about her. "Son of a gun," she whispered to herself. "Isn't that something. Isn't that nice."

Jake helped her to her feet and dusted her knees. "Isn't what nice?"

"Hmmm? Um, isn't it nice that no one's hurt."

Jake looked at her carefully. "You sure you're okay? Your apartment just burned to a crisp, and you're grinning from ear to ear like the Cheshire Cat."

"I know. I can't help it." Berry pushed her mouth together with her fingers, trying to wipe away the smile. "I'll try to look more serious."

Mrs. Fitz dabbed at her nose with a tissue. "Lingonberry, I'm so sorry. It was all my fault. I got a nice big tip for delivering those pizzas, and I spent it on some newfangled electronic curlers, and the dang things burned the apartment up."

Berry looked to Jake. "Is that true? Is that how the fire started?"

Jake nodded. "Mrs. Fitz plugged the curlers in to heat up, and then she set the case on the couch. Somehow, the curlers overheated and started to spark. The couch caught fire, then the curtain went up."

"How bad is it?"

"Could be worse. The fire was confined to the couch area. Mostly what you've got is smoke damage. The downstairs wasn't affected at all."

"Can I go in?"

"Yeah. I just went through with the fire marshall. They're packing up to leave. You'll have to go down to the fire station later to fill out some forms."

Berry nodded and led the little parade of three ladies and Jake Sawyer up the stairs to her apartment. She walked into the middle of the living room, her feet squishing across the wet carpet, and blinked into the darkness. Everything was charcoal gray. The walls, the ceilings, the rugs, the windows. The couch looked like it had been burned to cinders by the fire, stomped into oblivion by overzealous firefighters, and drowned. "Oh, dear."

"It makes a body want to cry to see it like this," Mrs. Fitz said. "It was so cozy."

"It'll never be the same," Mrs. Dugan sniffed. "It smells. Everything in here smells, all our clothes, all the linens, all the tea bags."

Berry wrinkled her nose. "It is pretty stinky. Tomorrow morning we'll open the windows and try to air it out."

"Maybe we should go back to the train station for a while," Mildred offered. "You could come with us, Lingonberry."

Jake gave a long-suffering, earth-rocking sigh. "Nobody's going to the train station. I have an empty house with plenty of space. You can all stay with me for a few days while we get the apartment cleaned."

Berry looked at him sidewise. "You sure you want to do this?"

"No. Yes."

"A house!" Mrs. Fitz elbowed Mrs. Dugan. "Hear that? We're gonna live in a house."

Mildred carefully squished across the room. "I'll get my toothbrush and my nightie." She stopped at the bathroom door and gasped. She plucked a dingy gray object off the sink and held it up for inspection. "Is this my toothbrush?" Tears filled her round eyes and made streaks down her sooty, wrinkled cheeks. "That's the last straw. Even my toothbrush."

Jake gathered the ladies in his arms and ushered them down the stairs. "We can get new toothbrushes. We can get new nighties. Let's just get out of here for now. Everything will look better in the morning."

Berry followed after them, wondering why she didn't feel depressed. Her apartment was a shambles. Anyone in her right mind would be sobbing her eyes out, but she felt like singing. It must be shock, she concluded. Some sort of bizarre reaction to tragedy.

She watched Jake's glossy black hair bob down the stairs in front of her, assessed his broad shoulders, admired his behind, and admonished herself to stop smiling. This was a serious situation. This called for a sober attitude. How would it look if she emerged from her charred apartment with a two-mile-wide grin plastered on her face? People might easily reach the wrong conclusion and suspect she wanted to live in Jake Sawyer's big old house. They might even suspect she wanted to live in Jake Sawyer's big old bed. She shook her head as if to clear it of the thought. How had such an idea even popped into her mind? She absolutely did not want to sleep with Jake Sawyer. And if she did, she would never admit it, not even to herself. "There," she said, "that's settled."

Jake held the downstairs door open. "What's settled? And why do you look so smug?"

"I don't look smug. I look depressed and worried about my apartment."

"If this is depressed, I can't wait to see you when you're happy." He locked the apartment door, put the CLOSED sign in the window of the Pizza

Place, and locked the front door. "I got a rental car today. It's just down the block."

Berry looked at the tan station wagon. "A station wagon? You don't seem like the station wagon type."

Jake helped Mrs. Dugan climb into the back seat. "I don't know what type I am. One minute I'm a carefree bachelor, riding high on Gunk . . . then all of a sudden I've got a houseful of women. And none of them are any good for bachelor-type pursuits."

Berry rammed her hands onto her hips. "What's that supposed to mean? What do I look like? Chopped liver?"

Jake's eyes traveled the length of her in mock appraisal. She narrowed her eyes as he studied her unruly curls, her turned-up little nose, her mouth that was compressed into a thin line of irritation. His eyes moved to her throat, her tan safari shirt, her small, round breasts. Berry gritted her teeth and wished for cleavage. She'd never cried about cleavage before, but for some inexplicable reason she wanted some now. "Are you laughing at me?" she snapped.

"Maybe a little."

He continued his assessment with slow leisure, dallying at the zipper on her jeans, and finally concluding with a cursory glance at her running shoes. When he raised his eyes back to hers there was still laughter, but there was something else as well. Something that made her toes curl in her shoes and her heart thump under her breastbone. She decided it was something even more flammable than defective curlers.

Jake tugged at a yellow curl. "I'm afraid, Lingonberry, that you are very much like your name: delicious but virtually unobtainable. You would not be the first choice of a carefree bachelor. You are definitely wife material."

Berry inelegantly plopped onto the front seat. "I don't know if I've just been insulted or complimented."

Jake started the car and pulled away from the curb. He reached across the seat, taking her hand in his, rubbing his thumb erotically across the sensitive flesh of her palm. "You've been complimented."

The smile returned to the corners of her mouth, and a warm glow radiated from her heart. It had been a lot of years since she'd received a compliment from a man. She'd almost forgotten how nice it could be. When she reached her objective of a successful business and a college degree, she was definitely going to find time to look for a complimenting husband. She'd add that to her list of postponed pleasures . . . just after butterscotch pudding. At the very top of the pleasure list would be a man with great thumbs. Jake had great thumbs. They were massaging little circles on the inside of her wrist, encouraging mental images of more intimate thumb activities. *Good grief.* Berry blushed, withdrawing her hand. *Shame on me.*

"Hey, look at this," Mrs. Fitz exclaimed, "we're out in the country. Isn't this something?"

"This isn't the country," Mrs. Dugan said. "This is the suburbs. You can tell the difference because the suburbs haven't got cows. There are cows in the country."

Berry tried to relax as the scenery on Ellenburg Drive flew by. Cows or not, in her book this was country. There were pretty houses, tucked back off the road with lots of space between them. There were lots of big trees and barking dogs. The road narrowed to cross a good-sized creek and then began to snake uphill to Jake Sawyer's house. Berry felt as if she was going on vacation. She hadn't been on a vacation in six years, but going on vacation was like riding a bike—you never forgot the feeling.

There was a sense of expectation in the car. The air over the back seat fairly crackled with it as the ladies leaned forward in hushed anticipation, and in the front seat Berry couldn't have been more excited if she was spending a week at St. Moritz. She hugged herself and grinned. There would be lots of peace and quiet, and crickets chirping, and trees whooshing in the wind, and Jake Sawyer in his underwear.

Berry's mind snapped to attention. She sat up straighter in her seat. *Hold it. Replay that tape. Jake Sawyer in his underwear. Damn.* She had a vision of Jake Sawyer in his sexy blue briefs. It was stuck in her brain like the refrain of a song that refused to be forgotten. Jake Sawyer in his underwear. How do you forget something like that?

Berry bit her lip, silently groaned, and rolled her window down a crack. It was getting warm in the car. This would never do. She had to put all this into proper perspective. This was not a vacation. And this was certainly not going to include Jake Sawyer in his you-know-what.

Mrs. Fitz poked her in the shoulder. "Are we almost there?"

"Yes," Berry snapped, "and this is not a vacation."

Mrs. Fitz shook her head. "What a ninny. Of course it's a vacation."

Berry sighed and slumped in her sat. This was going to be tough.

The house looked smaller and much less menacing by daylight. In fact, Berry decided, it was downright cheerful. The house was bordered by dormant flowerbeds and a broad lawn. Several oak trees pressed their limbs towards the yellow siding. The lawn was surrounded by a buffer of woods. The white gingerbread trim sparkled in the sunshine. The front door was carved oak and topped with a stained glass window.

Mrs. Fitz gave a long, low whistle. "This is a pip of a house."

Berry stood in the foyer and admired the freshly waxed hardwood flooring, the hand-carved cherry banister that spiraled up the stairs, the ornate door jambs. The entire downstairs had been painted a creamy white, giving the house a light, airy feeling. It contained few pieces of furniture. A large overstuffed buff-colored couch and matching club chair had been placed at the perimeters of an Oriental area rug in the living room. A pottery table lamp sat on the floor next to the chair. The foyer opened into a breakfast area at the rear of the house. A large round butcher-block table nestled into the curve of a long bay window. It was a great house, Berry admitted. Worth every cent of his Gunk money. And it deserved to have a terrific car sitting in its garage. She felt a true pang of remorse for the loss of the Gunk car. The car and the house belonged together.

"This is gonna be fun," Mrs. Fitz said. "I always wanted to live in a house like this. Boy, this feels like home. I could stay here forever. Come on, ladies, let's go upstairs and explore."

Berry caught the look of horror that passed through Jake's eyes and had to clap her hand over her mouth to keep from giggling.

Jake grabbed her by the nape of her neck, sending delicious shivers clear to her toes. "I saw that smile. You've got a mean streak in you, Lingonberry Knudsen." His thumb massaged small circles on her neck just below her ear, and his muscled thigh grazed against her denim-clad leg.

Berry's eyes glazed over with the sheer pleasure of his touch.

Jake put his mouth to her ear and spoke in a husky whisper. "She wouldn't really stay here forever, would she?"

"Mmmmm," Berry purred, "mmmmaybe."

"I like Mrs. Fitz, but I'd slit my throat if I thought she was going to stay forever."

Berry stared at his throat and wondered if he'd mind if she nibbled on it. Jake Sawyer looked entirely edible, and he smelled wonderfully masculine—like musk cologne and campfire. Oh, lord, Berry thought, he doesn't smell like campfire, he smells like charcoal-roasted couch. Back to reality. This is not a vacation. This is not a romantic encounter.

Jake plunged his hands into his pockets and grinned at her. "Changed your mind?"

Berry blinked at him. "What do you mean?"

"For a minute there, you looked like you were contemplating nibbling on my neck."

"Jeez."

He stepped closer, backing Berry up against the foyer wall. "Just to get the record straight, I think I should tell you that it's okay for you to nibble on my neck any time you want. It isn't as if we're strangers, you know. After all, you have seen me in my underwear . . ."

Berry stared at him in stoic resignation. They were back to his underwear. This was never going to work. He had an evil sense of humor, he read minds, and he gave her a hormone attack just by lowering his voice an octave. "I think I should go home," Berry said, inwardly wincing when her voice cracked on the word home.

Jake shook his head. "Tsk, tsk, tsk. Where's your sense of adventure? Don't you want to be bold, like a red geranium?" His voice was teasing, but his eyes were serious, and the sexual tension stretched taut between them.

Berry gnawed on her lower lip. "Geraniums aren't in bloom yet. And neither am I," she added. "We're out of season."

Jake grinned. His eyes focused on her mouth. He moved two inches closer, and Berry felt the panic rise in her throat as the tips of her breasts crushed against the wall of his chest. Oh, Lordy, she thought with a gasp, he's going to kiss me. He's going to plant those incredible lips of his on mine and melt the soles of my sneakers. She didn't know whether to close her eyes and pray it didn't happen, or leave her eyes open so she wouldn't miss a single thing. Jake lowered his mouth to hers before she had a chance to make a decision. It was a short, gentle kiss. A tender claiming of her mouth.

"Are you blooming, yet?" he whispered against her lips, a hint of laughter mingled with raspy impatience.

Blooming? She was bursting! She listened to the pounding of her heart and wondered about the statistics on twenty-six-year-old women having heart attacks while necking.

She watched the laughter leave his eyes as he studied her reaction. He ran his finger across her lower lip and tangled his hand in her hair. When he kissed her this time it was with barely checked passion. His tongue hungrily searched out sweet secrets, causing Berry's stomach to tumble with each thrust, causing her to swell with the desire to be truly loved. She pressed her hips against his and moaned softly as a pleasurable ache spread through her.

Jake broke from the kiss and shakily held her at arm's length when he heard Mrs. Fitz come thumping down the stairs.

"Wait until you see the upstairs, Berry. It's wonderful," Mrs. Fitz exclaimed. "You can see forever from the third-floor windows."

Mrs. Dugan followed her. "Not much furniture in this house. No window shades. I can't live in a house without window shades."

Jake gestured to the cartons stacked along the dining room walls. "There are extra linens in one of those cartons. We can tack a couple of sheets up for tonight." He zipped his jacket and opened the front door. "I guess I'd better go buy some toothbrushes."

Four

Mrs. Fitz, Mrs. Dugan, and Mildred perched on the edge of the couch, their eyes glued to the television set, their mouths slightly open as they watched the last few minutes of *Ghostbusters* on the VCR. Scattered in front of them were the remnants of supper: Styrofoam hamburger cartons, a few ketchup-soaked french fries, five empty milkshake containers, and a large bakery box containing one lonely doughnut.

Berry sat on the rug, her back resting against the edge of the couch. A gigantic marshmallow man had just appeared on the screen, and Berry decided he didn't seem nearly so menacing as Jake Sawyer stoking the fire in the Franklin stove. Jake wore jeans that seductively clung to the most mouth-watering buns Berry had ever seen. Definitely not the buns of a chemist, she concluded. It would be a sin to hide them under a lab coat and sequester them in a stuffy lab all day. Jake Sawyer had the buns of a pirate. Rogue buns. Her eyes glazed over in silent appreciation while she memorized the contours and speculated on the hidden details. When Jake stood and stretched, she quickly transferred her attention to the movie.

She sensed, rather than saw, Jake moving towards her. His knee grazed against her shoulder and Berry knew if she turned her head she'd be staring into the intriguing bulge behind his zipper—the one part of his anatomy that was possibly more perfect than his behind. Don't look! she warned her eyes. You know what trouble you got into last time you ogled that bulge!

He nudged her again with his knee, more firmly this time, pushing her forward a bit. "Scoot up," he whispered.

Before Berry knew what had happened she felt him slide behind her, sandwiching himself into a sitting position between her and the couch, trapping her between his legs. She inched forward, but he wrapped an arm around her waist, holding her secure against his chest. His voice hummed softly into her hair. "This is nice."

Nice? Nice was a little bland for what she felt. What she felt was more like *WOW* and *HOLY TOLEDO.* Unfortunately, this was not the time for *WOW* feelings. Her life was complicated enough. She could barely hold her own between the Pizza Place and her studies, and it kept getting worse. First the ladies, then the jeep, now the fire. She couldn't imagine what would happen next, but she was damn well going to make sure it wasn't a broken heart. "I don't think this is a good idea."

"Shhh, the movie. You'll disturb the ladies."

Berry looked to the ladies but found them engrossed in the heroics of Bill Murray. She wriggled within Jake's grasp, attempting to free herself.

"Lord, Berry, now you're disturbing me. Will you stop sliding around? This is going to get embarrassing."

She carefully relaxed into his chest and sat perfectly still, not wanting to encourage anything, but secretly enjoying her ability to arouse him. It was a good thing she was in a room with three little old ladies, she thought, because she was getting entirely too much pleasure from the warm intimacy of Jake's embrace. His steady heartbeat vibrated throughout her body, rain had begun to splash against the dark windows of the cozy Victorian, and the marshmallow ghost exploded.

Mrs. Dugan's eyes shone with excitement as the credits rolled across the screen. "First time I've ever seen a VCR. It's a wonderful thing."

Mrs. Fitz agreed. "It was a treat."

Jake eased away from Berry. "Speaking of treats, I have some goodies to distribute." Two minutes later he returned from the kitchen with an armful of shopping bags. "Mrs. Fitz, this belongs to you. Mrs. Dugan, here's your loot." He handed a bag to Mildred.

"Lipstick!" Mrs. Fitz announced. "He bought me lipstick. And a nightgown." She held it up for inspection. "It's a pip."

"Here's the toothbrushes," Mildred smiled shyly. "This is better than Christmas. We got slippers, and face cream, and hairbrushes."

Berry looked at Jake. "You're awfully good at buying women's toiletries."

"I have four younger sisters. I know all about girl things," he told her proudly.

Mildred stifled a yawn, "I can't wait to get into my nightgown and climb into bed." She looked questioningly at Jake. "Where is my bed?"

Jake stuffed his hands into his jeans pockets. "I have four bedrooms, but only one bed. I suppose the most sensible arrangement is for you ladies to use my king-size bed. Berry and I will sleep downstairs."

Mrs. Dugan narrowed her eyes. "You're not planning any funny stuff, are you? I won't put up with hanky-panky."

"The thought never entered my mind. Berry can sleep on the couch, and I'll rough it on the floor. I have some sleeping bags upstairs."

Mrs. Dugan pressed her lips together. "I suppose that will be all right, but I've got good ears. You better watch your step."

Jake's face creased into a good-natured smile. "Yes, ma'am."

Berry watched the women climb the stairs. "That was really nice of you to get lipstick and face cream for them. It's been a long time since they could afford those luxuries."

"You haven't opened your bag."

Berry studied the pale lavender bag on the coffee table. It was smaller than everyone else's bag, and it was from an expensive shop catering to fancy lingerie and expensive perfume. It was a bag designed to hold silk teddies and black lace garter belts. "I'm afraid to open it. Is this something extravagant?"

"Sleepwear."

She extracted a small bottle of perfume that she suspected cost more than a replacement for her jeep. "Umm . . . there's only perfume in here."

"Yup."

"Everyone else got flannel nightgowns."

"Isn't there a nightgown in there?"

Berry searched the tiny bag. "No."

Jake stroked her cheek with his fingertip. His eyes grew the color of strong coffee. His voice turned alarmingly husky. "You're so beautiful with your unruly blond curls and silky peaches-and-cream skin. You should wear nothing to bed but a dab of expensive perfume between your breasts

. . . and possibly a dab in one other very intimate place." His hands traced the slender column of her neck and rested in a caress on her shoulders. "I have a confession to make. I'm in big trouble here. I'm having heart problems."

"Good lord. What kind of heart problems?"

"Heartache, heartthrob, heart flutters. I feel like the Grinch at Christmas—you know, the part where his heart grew two sizes in one day. And I thought my heart was going to stop when I saw you for the first time, lying on the ground beneath that big old oak tree. You looked like a slightly dotty modern-day wood nymph."

Berry's eyes flew open. "Slightly dotty?"

"For crying out loud, you were flat out on a pizza." He grinned at her indignation and cuddled her close to him. "Maybe someday you'll develop heart problems, and you'll come to me wearing just two dabs of perfume."

"No way. No, sir. Nothing doing."

He curled his fingers in her hair, holding her head captive while he lowered his mouth to hers and kissed her slowly and gently. It was like being drugged, Berry thought. Once he was this close to her she was a goner. Her thinking slowed, and her heart rate accelerated. At the first touch of his tongue her stomach tumbled. He was pressing himself into her belly, cupping her buttocks so she couldn't escape the feel of him wanting her.

"I'm going to tell Mrs. Dugan on you," Berry murmured halfheartedly.

"Mrs. Dugan doesn't scare me."

"Oh, ha!"

"Okay, maybe a little." He kissed her again, much more urgently this time, opening the two top buttons on her shirt, exposing a soft swell of breast, diping his finger inside the lace cup to seek the small excited nipple.

Berry gasped at the hot tingle his touch provoked. Her eyelids felt heavy, her blood thick with desire. He rhythmically moved his hips so the hardness of him rubbed across the zipper of her jeans, causing passion to churn through her body. What was it about this man that provoked such a volatile reaction? She'd felt it the first moment she saw him. She wanted Jake Sawyer. She wanted him with a ferocity that ripped apart her best intentions and tested the standards she'd set for her own sexual morality. She slid her hands down his back to the waistband of his jeans, splaying her fingers across his slim hips, wanting to touch him—needing to know him more intimately.

The kiss was no longer playful. The tongue that had been sensuously sliding along Berry's lips thrust deep into her mouth in a hungry parody of entry that Berry accepted and returned. She moaned softly as his hands covered her breasts, releasing the front snap on her bra, exposing her turgid nipples to his marauding mouth, and Berry felt herself floating in a musky haze of delicious, aching sensations.

A pattering of slippered feet upstairs and a fit of obtrusive coughing pierced the haze and attracted Berry's attention. "We're going to bed now," Mrs. Fitz called down. "Anybody need anything from the bedroom?"

Berry looked at Jake in dazed frustration. "What? Oh, hell."

Jake's exclamation wasn't nearly so polite. He pulled his shirttails out of his jeans and arranged himself. "Don't want to alarm the ladies."

Berry looked at it and smiled shakily. It was going to take more than shirttails to disguise his response to her.

Jake returned with two sleeping bags draped over his arm and a large royal-blue silk pajama top in his hand. He dropped the sleeping bags on the floor and held the pajama top up for Berry's inspection. "My sister Amy gave me these pajamas last Christmas. She has an enhanced image of bachelor existence."

"Mmmm?"

"I'd prefer you only wear the perfume to bed, but if you're the shy type you could start out in these."

Berry took the pajama top and narrowed her eyes. "To begin with, where's the other half? You only brought me the top."

"I thought the bottoms would get in our way."

"Read my lips. I am not going to bed with you."

"You would have if Mrs. Fitz hadn't interrupted."

"A moment of weakness. It won't happen again. Maybe I'll just sleep in my clothes."

"Don't you think that will be uncomfortable?"

Berry couldn't think of anything more uncomfortable than sleeping in Jake's silky pajamas. The very idea gave her a lust attack. She chose one of the sleeping bags and laid it the length of the couch.

Jake watched her, amusement twitching at the corners of his mouth. "They zip together, you know."

"Not tonight, they don't."

He began to undress, slowly and deliberately, in full view of her.

"What are you doing?" she croaked.

"Getting undressed for bed."

"Aren't you going to turn off the light? Aren't you going to wear pajamas? Don't you have to brush your teeth, or something?"

"Nope."

"Terrific." She jumped into her sleeping bag and turned her face to the back of the couch.

"I thought you liked watching men undress."

"Monster," she hissed. A male striptease! She felt a rivulet of perspiration trickle down between her breasts and wasn't sure if it was from embarrassment, frustration, or the down-filled sleeping bag. She gave an annoyed grunt.

"Aren't you going to look?"

Berry gnashed her teeth together at Jake's soft laughter. Why was he so relaxed about all this when she was sweating like a pig? Why wasn't he nervous? Jake Sawyer was entirely too comfortable about sexy kisses and nakedness. Jake Sawyer probably had more girl friends than Quaker had oats.

Jake padded quietly across the room to shut off the light. "Last chance to look," he offered in a loud whisper.

"Oh! Ugh!"

Another soft chuckle and the room was plunged into darkness. Berry listened to him position his own bag as close as possible to the couch. There was a rustle of material and the sound of a zipper. In a short time the room was filled with quiet regular breathing. He was asleep. What nerve!

Berry lay absolutely rigid, furious because Jake Sawyer had fallen asleep instantly, and she was wide awake. She peeked over the side of the couch and watched him. He was wickedly tasty-looking, and she had to admit, he really did bring out her voyeuristic tendencies. He also was beginning to bring out other tendencies—like maternal instincts, wifely musings, and lonely dissatisfactions. There was more to this than sex, Berry realized, sighing. True, there was an instant magnetism between them, but it would have died a quick death if she hadn't liked him. He was kind. He was fun. He was brave. She liked him.

She tapped his bare shoulder.

"Mmmm?"

"Jake, are you awake?"

"I am now."

"Why do you want to make love with me?"

There was a soft groan. "You woke me up to ask me that?"

"Uh . . . yeah."

"I don't know. I guess it's like asking someone why they want to climb a mountain, and they say because it's there."

"What?" She made an attempt to get to her feet, forgetting she was in the confining sleeping bag. "Oh, hell!" She rolled off the couch and crashed down on top of him.

"Oooof!"

Berry stared into his eyes. "Are you okay?"

"Some women will do anything to get on top."

Berry punched him in the chest and ungracefully slithered off. "You're impossible. Big, dumb, macho male."

"I'm not dumb."

"That was a dumb answer."

"Okay, wait a minute. I'll think of a better one."

"Too late. You only get one chance." She was falling for him, the stupid oaf. Here she was getting cravings to iron his shirts, and he was thinking of her as a mountain to climb. Of all the rotten luck. She climbed back onto the couch.

"Berry . . ."

"Don't talk to me."

SLAM!

Berry awoke with a jolt and sat up in her sleeping bag.

STOMP, STOMP, STOMP.

Jake opened one eye and looked at Berry. "We have elephants upstairs? The circus come in to town last night while I was sleep?"

"I think the ladies are up."

Jake looked at his watch. "It's five-twenty."

The lights flashed on upstairs, and footsteps sounded on the stairs.

Jake groaned and unzipped his bag. Berry caught a flash of white thigh in the darkened living room and focused her eyes on the ceiling until she heard the zip of his fly.

Jake switched the light on and Mrs. Fitz stood blinking at them. She wore her new flannel night-gown and pink furry slippers, and six inches of grey frizz stood straight out from her head.

"Lord," Jake whispered to Berry, "she looks like she's been electrocuted."

Berry bit her lip. "Something wrong, Mrs. Fitz?"

"I need tea," she growled and shuffled off towards the kitchen.

Next, Mrs. Dugan stomped down the stairs, gave Berry and Jake a cursory glance, and huffed after Mrs. Fitz. There was a flurry of banging pots and clattering silverware from the kitchen. A few minutes later Mildred joined them.

Jake stood with his hands on his hips and a grin on his face. "I don't think the ladies had a good night."

Berry gave him a black look. The ladies weren't the only ones who didn't have a good night. The man was a menace. And he wasn't wearing any underwear. His briefs were indecently lying next to his shirt and socks. He stood barefooted and bare-chested, wearing nothing but his faded jeans, slung low on his perfect hips. There was some-thing very disturbing about that. It made Berry feel hot and scratchy in private places. She unconsciously stared at him, wondering what it felt like to have denim rub against your . . .

"Where's the tea bags?" Mrs. Fitz called crankily. "I can't find nothing in this kitchen."

Jake shook his head and sauntered out to the kitchen. Soon soothing sounds drifted in to Berry. Jake was telling Mrs. Fitz how nice she looked in the morning . . . full of energy. Mrs. Dugan and Mildred were similarly pacified. A tablecloth was discovered and spread over the round oak table. A blue tea pot appeared. Packing crates were drawn up to serve as chairs.

Berry joined the women at the table. She thought Mrs. Fitz was beginning to come around, but Mildred looked like death. Her red-rimmed eyes sagged in her face, and her mouth crinkled into a small furrow in pasty cheeks. "Mildred, do you feel all right?"

Mildred slumped against the table, staring glassy-eyed at her tea cup. "Couldn't sleep all night. Didn't sleep a wink."

Mrs. Fitz looked disgusted. "You snored all night, you old bat. And you hogged the pillow."

Mrs. Dugan leaned across the table. "You! You were the one who hogged the pillow. Tossing and turning and complaining. Mildred was the perfect bed partner compared to you."

Jake deposited a steaming mug of coffee in front of Berry. "Looks like we have a problem here."

"Possible multiple homicides."

"I think I'll go out and rent some beds today." He slouched over Berry, draping his bare arm across her collarbone, and whispered in her ear. "I only have four bedrooms. Guess that means two of us will have to double up."

Mrs. Dugan glared at him. "I heard that. You men. You only have one thing on your mind. Sex. Sex. Sex."

Mrs. Fitz winked at Jake. "Don't pay no attention to her. She's cranky because she's always got sex on her mind, too, but she can't remember what you're supposed to do about it. Last man Mrs. Dugan knew was old Criswald, and he couldn't remember what to do about it either."

Mildred giggled. Mrs. Dugan looked scandalized. Mrs. Fitz looked like she was enjoying their reactions. "I tell you what." She smiled broadly. "How about when Jake goes out to rent us some beds, he rents us some handsome men to go with them?"

Sara Dugan pursed her lips. "That's disgusting."

"Yeah. But it made Mildred giggle. It's bringing some color to her cheeks."

Berry sipped at her coffee and thought she wouldn't want to underestimate Mrs. Fitz. Her methods were a bit unorthodox for a little old lady, but she knew how to rally the troops.

Jake made an effort at controlling his laughter and finished his coffee. "It's Saturday. What time does the Pizza Place open on Saturday?"

"Ten."

"I guess we can get ourselves together by ten."

"First breakfast," Mrs. Dugan offered.

"Then we do the laundry." Mrs. Fitz drained her cup of tea. "If we don't do the laundry we'll have to work in our nighties."

Jake set his cup on the table and lazily stretched behind Berry. "I'll take a quick shower, and then we can check out the apartment."

Berry was having a difficult time not bursting into tears. The apartment was even worse than she'd remembered. The soot was everywhere. It had infiltrated every drawer, it clung to the walls, and it blackened the windows.

Jake put his arms around Berry and rested his chin on the top of her head. "You're not going to cry, are you?"

"No. Absolutely not." A large tear rolled down her cheek.

Jake wiped it away with his thumb. "I hate when you cry. It gives me a lump in my throat."

"Everything is ruined."

"Not everything."

Berry looked down at the rug. "The rug is ruined."

"Mmmm." His voice rumbled in her ear.

Berry was having a difficult time concentrating on the rug. She was being distracted by his hands inching their way down her spine. "And the couch is ruined."

"Mmmm. The couch." The hands squeezed her ever so slightly and his thumbs massaged little circles into her back just above the waistband of her jeans.

"And . . . um." She couldn't think what else was ruined. It was right on the tip of her tongue, but she was being rendered senseless by his thumbs.

"It's not so bad," Jake cooed. "The curlers were faulty and the company will be responsible for damages, including cleanup. I think we should gather up the clothes and linens and take them all back to my house to be washed. The rest of this you can leave to the professionals."

Berry squeezed her eyes shut and another tear popped out. "It makes me sad to see it like this."

"Me, too."

"I think I'd feel better if I cleaned it a little."

"Me, too."

"Really?"

"No, but I'll do anything to prevent another tear from sliding down your cheek." He turned and rummaged through the drawers by the sink. "Where are your big garbage bags?"

"One drawer down."

He located the bags and tossed them to her. "Here you go. Stuff the clothes and linens in these. I'm going to get the rug up before it ruins the floor."

Berry filled the station wagon with the bagged laundry and looked up at her open windows. Jake was stuffing part of the waterlogged rug through one of them. "Bombs away," he called, catapulting the rug onto the sidewalk below.

"Jake?"

He leaned out the window and grinned. His shirt sleeves were rolled to above the elbow, and a black smudge slanted across his cheek.

"Thanks."

"Are you looking for a way to show gratitude?"

Berry smiled in spite of herself. She had to admire his tenacity.

An hour later Berry returned with Mrs. Fitz and Mildred. She unlocked the door to the Pizza Place and was relieved to see only a few water stains creeping down the walls.

"Just as good as new," Mrs. Fitz commented.

Mildred set a bunch of wildflowers on the counter. "I picked these this morning in the woods behind Jake's house. Don't they look nice?"

Berry smelled the flowers. "They look great."

Mrs. Fritz wrapped a snow-white apron around her ample middle. "We can handle this. You go on upstairs and help Jake with the apartment. Sounds like he's having a party up there."

Berry wrinkled her nose. It did sound like a party upstairs. There was music blaring from a radio and the sound of at least a dozen feet scuffing around. She took the stairs two at a time and found her apartment filled with people. Mrs. Giovanni stood at the sink, up to her elbows in soapsuds. Several adult Lings were scrubbing walls and scouring floors. Ling children ran from bedroom to living room in a game of tag. A tall black man turned from a sparkling-clean front window. He held a bottle of glass cleaner and looked pleased. "They're pretty clean, now. Now you can see Mama Giovanni's geraniums and down the street my Caribe Restaurant."

Berry caught Jake by the arm as he hauled a load of trash to the stairs. "What are all these people doing here?"

"They just showed up, one by one. You were right. This is a nice neighborhood."

"They came to help me?"

"Mrs. Ling said you were the reason her daughter won her class spelling bee last month. Said you tutored her free for weeks before the contest. Mrs. Giovanni tells me you drove her to the hospital every day for almost a month this winter when her husband had a heart attack."

"The black man," she whispered. "I've never met him."

"Apparently you've befriended his wife."

Berry looked confused.

"Anne Marie."

Berry's eyes opened wide. "Anne Marie?" She burst out laughing. "Anne Marie is a six-foot-tall platinum blonde who only speaks French. She gets lonely when her husband is at work, so she visits me. I speak English and make pizzas, and she sits on the stool, knitting and speaking French. Neither of us can understand anything the other says."

Jake shook his head. "How can you find time to

do all these things, run a business, and go to school?"

"I've eliminated sleeping and only eat once a day."

Jake was serious. "What about time for Berry?"

"I like my life."

"I think you're running on empty. When you say you haven't got time for naked men—you're right."

"Naked men do not play an important role in my life."

Jake grinned down at her. "I intend to change that."

"Good thing for you Mrs. Dugan stayed home to do the laundry. I'd tell her you were talking dirty to me."

"That isn't talking dirty." He leaned forward and whispered some of his future intentions in her ear. He stepped back, grinning, enjoying the look of flustered embarrassment on her face. "Now *that's* talking dirty."

Mrs. Giovanni bustled past with a bottle of detergent in her hand. She shook her finger at Berry. "You got a nice young man there. You're lucky to have a man like that to take care of you."

Jake whispered conspiratorily in Berry's ear. "See, even Mrs. Giovanni thinks I should take care of you."

"I don't need taking care of."

"Of course you do."

"Not the way you mean."

"Especially the way I mean."

Berry narrowed her eyes and put her fists on her hips. "I guess I know what I need and what I don't need. And I don't need what you think I need. I'm perfectly capable of taking care of myself."

"I suppose you are—but it would be much more fun if we did it together."

"I didn't mean . . . you know perfectly well . . . oh, forget it!"

Jake handed her the bag of trash. "Here, this isn't heavy. It's scraps of wallpaper I scraped off the bedroom wall. You could take it downstairs for me. It'll give you a chance to cool off." He winked at Mrs. Giovanni. "Just being around me gets her all overheated."

Berry took the bag and smacked Jake over the head with it. "Overheated," she muttered, trudging down the stairs. "I knew the man was a menace the minute I laid eyes on him. Pushy smart aleck. Damn him and his alarming body."

Mrs. Fitz stood in the doorway of the Pizza Place and clicked her tongue at Berry. "You look like someone just stepped on your corns."

"It's that Jake Sawyer."

"Isn't he something? Um-hmmm."

"The man has one thing on his mind."

"You?"

"S-e-x."

Mrs. Fitz looked at Berry. "Don't underestimate him."

Berry raised her eyebrows in question.

"He's in love with you."

"We hardly know each other."

"Sometimes your heart knows stuff your head hasn't figured out yet."

"He's never told me."

"Maybe he don't know. Maybe he knows, but he's afraid . . . like you."

Berry squared her shoulders. "I'm not afraid."

"Don't tell fibs."

"It's just that I have this plan . . ."

"Bullshoot."

"Mrs. Fitz! Such language."

Mrs. Fitz laughed and slapped her thigh. "I know it. Aren't I the ornery old lady, cussing like that?" She shook her head and returned to the caldron of pizza sauce bubbling on the stove. "You gotta be flexible, Lingonberry. Sometimes plans gotta change or you loose good opportunities. Isn't every day a man like Jake Sawyer comes along. That man is *fine*."

Mildred kneaded a huge wad of dough on the butcher-block table. A small smile hovered at her mouth. Her eyes twinkled. "And he's got great buns," she added quietly.

Five

Berry summoned her last ounce of strength and dragged herself out of the car. She glanced into the window of the Pizza Place, noticing that it was empty, except for Jake. Thank God. She didn't have the energy to be nice to any more customers. She pushed through the heavy glass door, tossed the money bag onto the counter and slumped into a chair. "Another day, another dollar."

Jake gaped at her. "You look awful!"

Berry pointed to her wet ringlets and water-splattered shirt. "Water balloon." She raised her leg to display torn jeans. "Dog."

"Does this happen every night?"

"Some nights are worse than others. Where are the ladies?"

"I sent them home in a cab. They looked all done in." He took her hands and pulled her to her feet. "You look even doner. Let's go home."

"I have to clean the ovens, the floor—"

Jake pointed vehemently. "To the car, woman!"

Berry was to tired to argue. She followed Jake to the car and sat beside him, remembering the way he'd said "Let's go home" as if it really were her home, too. Wouldn't that be nice, she thought, succumbing to the hypnotic drone of the engine. Imagine if that lovely Victorian house could actually be my home. It's nice to see Mrs. Giovanni's geraniums, but Jake's house has trees and a real lawn. She closed her eyes and imagined what it would be like to be barefoot on that lawn. No responsibilities, no plan to follow . . . just bare toes and soft grass.

When Berry opened her eyes she was in the garage.

"Come on, sleepyhead," Jake crooned. "We're home."

Berry looked at him drowsily. There was that word again. When Jake Sawyer said "home" it took on spiritual proportions. Home was an ark: a refuge against flood, pestilence and rude drivers, a haven for the harried, a cure for the sexually deprived.

Berry followed Jake into the kitchen and wondered what it was that made this house so homey. It was empty of furniture. Voices echoed in rooms not yet softened by curtains or carpets. By all standards the old building should have felt inhospitable. But it didn't—it felt like a home. Berry could practically smell butterscotch pudding cooling on the counter.

Suddenly the ghosts of crushed dreams tugged unmercifully at her heart. Dreams of towheaded children getting tucked into bed at night, dreams of a husband who nuzzled her neck in the kitchen and told her important things, like "I took the car to get a new muffler today." She'd entered into marriage anticipating a family, fantasizing about a big old house that would be filled with noisy love and security taken for granted. What a dope she'd been to look for domestic bliss in a marriage to Allen. It had never really been a marriage at all. It had been a living arrangement. She'd expected so much, and she'd left with so little.

She chewed on her lower lip. No, that wasn't entirely honest. The dissolution of her marriage wasn't a totally barren experience. She'd walked out on her emotionally shallow husband with renewed self-esteem and a hard-won sense of purpose. Somehow, an individual had emerged from the muddle of matrimony. She was proud of that.

"Looks like some heavy thinking going on behind those pretty blue eyes."

Berry's heart stopped for a second, afraid that he'd read her mind. She struggled for something to say. "This house feels like it should be filled with children."

"I agree. It's going to be perfect for a pack of kids and a couple of floppy-eared dogs."

Berry stared at him in confusion. He didn't have kids, and he didn't have a dog. What was he telling her? Had he bought the house for someone else? An investment? Was he only living here temporarily? Lord, did he have a pregnant girlfriend in Spokane?

Jake leaned against the counter. "I have a plan."

"What sort of plan?"

"When was the last time you ate?"

Berry blinked at the change in the conversation. "Uh . . . I don't remember."

"Did you have supper?"

Berry flushed at the realization that she'd had a candy bar for supper. She'd intended to have a salad, but somehow she'd never gotten to it. "What's this got to do with your plan?"

"Nothing. Everything." Jake opened the refrigerator door. "There's not much food in here."

"So, I'm not the only one who forgets to eat."

"I've been eating out. Mostly at my sister's house.

She's only a few miles from here." He put a half gallon of milk on the counter and found a box of raisin bran in the overhead cupboard. "I've only got breakfast food." He located a spoon and poured her a bowl of cereal.

Berry aimlessly pushed the raisins around with her spoon. "I'm not sure I have the energy to eat this."

Without saying a word, Jake poured some milk into the blender. He added an egg and searched through a small box sitting on the counter, finally extracting two bottles. "A little vanilla, a dash of nutmeg," he told Berry. He whipped the mixture and poured the frothy, creamy liquid into a large glass. "Here. You don't have to chew this."

"It has a raw egg in it."

"Eggnog usually does."

"Hmmm." Berry cautiously sipped at it and licked a milk mustache off with the tip of her tongue. He had a plan. Swell. Another plan. The world needed one more plan.

Jake took the empty glass and put it in the dishwasher. He slung an arm around Berry and eased her toward the stairs. "Let's go to bed."

"Don't I sleep on the couch?"

"I had beds delivered today. The ladies all have their own rooms."

"And?"

"And you sleep in my room." He opened the door to his bedroom and motioned her in with a Sir Walter Raleigh flourish.

"Oh, no," she groaned, "not tonight, Jake. I'm too tired."

Jake grinned at her as he turned down the bed linens. "No. Not tonight. When I share a bed with you for the first time I want you wide awake and panting."

Berry stood blank-faced in front of him, too

tired to formulate a retort, her mind focusing on the fact that he'd said "*When* I share a bed with you," not *if.* Was it that inevitable?

He draped the royal-blue silk pajama top across her shoulders, kissed her on the tip of her nose, and left, closing the door behind him.

Berry surfaced through the drowse of sleep, stretching her legs, then her arms. She was in the biggest, most comfortable bed she'd ever slept in. "Yum," she sighed, rolling onto her back, feeling the delicious silk pajama top slide over her breasts. This was a lovely way to awaken, she decided. Slowly and luxuriously . . . if only she didn't have this peculiar feeling of being watched. The feeling crept along her neck and tingled in her scalp. She cautiously opened one eye.

"Morning." Jake grinned down at her.

Berry pulled the covers up to her neck. "What are you doing in here?"

"I need some clothes. Want to take a shower?"

Berry looked at him suspiciously. He had a towel slung over his shoulder. "Aren't you going to take a shower now?"

"Yup. But I'm a good guy. I'd be willing to share it with you."

"What a pal."

"I can do wonderful things with soapsuds."

"I don't think I want to hear this."

Jake sat on the edge of the bed and ran his finger along the blue silk collar. "God, you're desirable in the morning. Warm and sexy and all mussed up." He touched the satiny pajamas. "I like the way you feel under this material. Now I know why they make pajamas out of it. It never felt like this when it was on me."

Berry liked it, too. It was fun to wake up feeling pampered and feminine for a change.

He ran the material between his fingers. "You would feel like this in the shower, when you got all lathered with soap." The jesting tone had left his voice, and in its place was honest curiosity and blatant sexuality. "Do you like the way it feels when you lather yourself with soap? Do you ever pretend it's a man's hand that glides across all those sensitive peaks and valleys?"

"Uh . . ." Holy cow. No one had ever said anything like that to her before. Not even her husband. Especially not her husband!

Jake's desire was obvious in his dark eyes as his finger traced a trail over the small swell of her breast. "Can you feel my touch through the satin?"

Could she feel it? She was branded. There was something incredible carnal about his lazy exploration of her pajama-clad breast. She licked her lips in anticipation of his good-morning kiss. When it happened, it said good morning, *good golly!* A flash of heat rippled under the blue satin and Berry feverishly returned the kiss, opening her mouth to his impatient tongue, winding her fingers in his soft curls.

When Jake finally broke from the kiss his voice was tinged with wonder and his eyes filled with longing. "This is what it would feel like if we were in the shower together," he said, sliding the satin across breasts that were swollen with desire. "If your breasts were slick with soap, it would feel warm and slippery . . . just like this." His hand slid lower, over her belly, and rested on the fabric of her panties.

Berry couldn't think. She was hot and throbbing behind tight nipples, behind the swollen bud that pressed against her panties, against Jake's palm. She grasped his shirt with trembling hands and buried her flushed face in his chest. "I think we'd better stop," she whispered breathlessly. "I feel so out of control. I've never felt like this before."

"It's special, Berry. It's special because it's you and me."

"Yes, but it's more than that . . . it's, um, it's the first time I've ever, um, felt anything like this."

Jake stared at her in stunned silence. "Berry, you were married for four years. Didn't you ever make love?"

"It turned out that I gave love, and he took love, but we never *made* love. We went through the motions on a regular basis, but nothing ever happened for me." She rolled her eyes. "This is *so* awkward."

"I hope I never meet this guy. I don't think I could keep from flattening his nose."

"It wasn't entirely his fault. I was very young. Allen and I both thought marriage could be a panacea for our own problems. Allen was very smart. He had direction to his life. He wanted to be a doctor. There I was floundering through school, changing my major every semester, barely passing half my courses—and Allen walked into my life. He was like the calm in the center of a hurricane. Cool blue eyes, perfectly combed hair, always a crease in his trousers. I think, unconsciously, we each felt incomplete. I needed order and purpose; he was lacking emotion. I suppose we thought if we joined the two of us together we'd get a complete human being.

"Unfortunately, life doesn't work that way. Marriage intensified our problems. The longer we were married, the less sure I became of myself, and he grew more withdrawn, less communicative. When it became clear that the marriage was a failure, Allen began looking to other women for comfort." Berry shrugged. "Maybe cheating was a last ditch effort for him. Maybe he was trying to convince himself that he wasn't deficient."

"Maybe he was a creep."

Berry hugged her knees and laughed. "That was my original conclusion. Time and personal growth have softened the edges of my animosity."

Someone obtrusively clumped down the hall, stopping short of Jake's bedroom door. "Anyone wanting to use the bathroom should do it now," Mrs. Fitz hissed in a loud whisper. "They should get into the bathroom before Mrs. Dugan gets up."

Jake grinned. "You think she's trying to tell us something?"

Berry was the last to arrive at the breakfast table. She quietly slid onto a packing crate and poured a bowlful of cereal, being careful to avoid looking at Jake. She was practically senseless with embarrassment. She'd gone bonkers listening to him talk about soap. She couldn't have felt more exposed if she'd come to the breakfast table naked. She'd acted like a total sex fiend and then told him her life story. Lord, she was such a boob. She kept her eyes trained on the cereal without really seeing it. She added milk and stirred.

POW! A kernel of cereal flew past her ear. *POP, PING, POW.* Her cereal was exploding!

A kernel bounced off Mrs. Dugan's forehead. "I've been shot!" she cried. "Someone shot me in the forehead."

Mrs. Fitz dived under the table. "You haven't been shot, you old dunce. It's the cereal."

Jake jumped to his feet and clamped a dinner plate over the almost empty bowl.

"What is this stuff?" Berry gasped.

Jake cautiously removed the plate. The cereal

was bloated with milk, making soft snuffling noises. "I don't understand this. It never did this before. Maybe it was the way you were stirring it." He took the box of cereal and Berry's bowl and descended into the basement with them.

Mrs. Dugan shook her head. "This never happened when we lived in the Southside Hotel for Ladies."

Mrs. Fitz picked cereal out of her hair. "Yeah, that place was boring. Filled with old people." She shivered at the thought.

Mildred folded her napkin. "I like it here. I wish he hadn't taken that cereal away. I wanted to try some."

Berry stared at the cellar door, wondering what was down there. Dr. Jekyll's laboratory? Finally her curiosity grew stronger than her embarrassment. She excused herself from the table and cautiously opened the basement door. "Jake?"

"Mmmm."

"Can I come down? Will anything else explode?"

"Take your chances."

Berry looked around the cluttered well-lit room. Kites, model airplanes, wind socks and bicycle wheels hung from the ceiling. The walls were lined with bottle-laden shelves and crowded bulletin boards. Countertops held robot innards, computer equipment, and sacks of rice, whole wheat, and corn. There were toys everywhere: decapitated dolls, fuzzy bears, motorized skateboards, boxes of puzzles. Jake sat at a massive oak desk, intently staring at a soggy particle of cereal speared on a long skewer. Berry moved behind him. "I feel like I'm visiting Gyro Gearloose."

"Most of this stuff belongs to Katy's kids. I'm the toy fixer. The trouble is they break them a lot faster than I can fix them.." He looked around the room. "Some of this is mine. The kites and planes and wind socks are mine."

Berry looked sidewise at him. "You told me you didn't have any toys."

"I lied."

"What else have you lied about?"

Jake placed the skewer on his desk and turned in his chair to look at Berry. "I lied about my reasons for wanting to make love to you. You know, the mountain theory?"

Uh oh. Berry backed away from Jake. "Is this going to get erotic? Are you going to talk about soap?"

"So, soap turns you on, huh?"

"Certainly not."

Jake slouched in his chair, stretching his long legs in front of him, lacing his fingers behind his head. He grinned at Berry. "Don't you want to know my innermost motives? Don't you want to know about The Master Plan?"

"Well, yes." She shook her head. "No."

"Make up your mind."

"Don't get pushy."

Jake chuckled. "You're not very brave today."

"What a rotten thing to say! I'm almost always brave. I ate your stupid cereal, didn't I?"

"You were avoiding me. You poured that cereal without even looking at it."

"Did you give me that exploding cereal on purpose?"

Jake feigned indignance. *"Moi?"*

Berry sat on a tricycle. "Okay, so go ahead and tell me. What's this big plan you've got?"

Jake leaned forward, resting his elbows on the desk. His eyes darkened roguishly, and laugh lines crinkled in the corners. "We're going to get married, buy a couple of dogs, and have a whole bunch of kids. Maybe a hundred."

Berry jumped off the tricycle. "Are you nuts?"

"Well, okay . . . we don't have to have a hundred kids. I'm negotiable about the kids. One or two would be enough."

"No. Never. I don't want to get married. I've already been married, and I hated it. And if I did get married it wouldn't be to you. You would be the last man I'd marry." It was a lie, of course. She wanted to marry him so bad her teeth hurt. Berry crossed her fingers behind her back.

"Why don't you want to marry me? What's wrong with me?"

"Nothing's wrong with you. That's what's wrong."

Jake squinted slightly and wrinkled his nose. "You want to elaborate on that?"

"I have work to do. I don't have all day to stand here and talk about marriage. I have to make pizzas. I have to wash the floor. I have to study for an art history test." She started towards the stairs. "Could I borrow the car?"

"No. I'll drive you. It'll give us a chance to talk."

"I don't want to talk to you."

Jake made chicken sounds and flapped his arms. "Ugh."

Jake and Berry sat in the dark in the station wagon and glared at each other. Berry gritted her teeth. "I'm delivering this pizza."

"The hell you are. I'm delivering this pizza."

"It's my job, my Pizza Place, my pizza."

Jake looked at the dingy yellow brick apartment building. "It's ten o'clock at night, and that's a four-story walk-up in a lousy neighborhood. I'm not going to sit here cooling my heels while you're in some dark hallway quietly getting mugged."

"I've delivered pizzas here before."

"Good. Now it's my turn." He grabbed hold of the pizza box. "Lock the doors when I get out."

Berry grabbed the other side of the box and tugged. "You'll deliver this pizza when pigs fly."

Jake gasped and looked out the window. "Look at that!"

Berry strained to see what had caught his attention. "What?"

Jake jumped from behind the wheel with the pizza and slammed the door shut behind him. "Flying pigs," he called to Berry.

Berry narrowed her eyes. "Son of a beet!" She stomped into the building after Jake. "I hate being told what to do. Nobody can tell me what to do. This is my business. That was my pizza. And he wants to marry me. Ha! Fat chance."

She caught up with him as he was collecting the money. "If I wasn't so tired from all those stairs, I'd kick you in the knee."

"Gee, you're exciting when you talk physical like that."

Berry clenched her fists. "Humph."

"Too turned on to talk, huh?" He tweaked a blond curl and turned to the man standing in the door, holding his pizza. "She's crazy about me. Follows me everywhere." He slung an arm around Berry's shoulders and guided her down the stairs. "I know you're hot for my body, but you could have waited in the car."

"You wouldn't want to know what I'd like to do to your body."

"Is it kinky?"

"It's painful. Possibly terminal."

"I'm not really into pain." Jake opened the downstairs door and stared at the empty street. "Where's the car?"

•　　•　　•

It was almost one o'clock in the morning when Jake and Berry trudged through the front door of the house. They silently made their way to the kitchen and began fixing a midnight snack of gigantic proportions. They carried the contents of the refrigerator to the round oak table and in the silvery light of moonbeams scoffed down pickles, sandwiches, ice cream, potato salad, and a pint of strawberries.

Jake pushed away from the table while Berry picked at the last strawberry. "Honey?"

Berry sighed.

"It's okay. I'll rent a new car in the morning."

Another sigh.

"The police were pretty reasonable, considering that's the second car we've had stolen in less than a week."

"In less than a week I've squashed a jeep, I've had two cars stolen, and my apartment's been charbroiled. You think someone's trying to tell me something?"

Jake shrugged. "That's just the negative side. What about the plus side?"

"What have I got on the plus side?"

"Our friendship."

Berry looked at him. He was serious. She smiled. "Yeah. I guess I do." Berry was glad it was dark in the breakfast nook. For a brief second tears blurred her vision, and she knew the expression on her face was radiant. Her heart and soul were swelling with brand-new emotions. They were the emotions she should have felt for Allen, but never did.

She'd begun her marriage with the very best of intentions, but the emotions simply weren't there, and hard as she tried, she couldn't manufacture them. They were emotions that didn't even have names, only texture and feeling. A pleasant warmth deep within, a very small smile that refused to fade, a foolish euphoria. Jake Sawyer thought their friendship was important. *Imagine that.* She grinned, blinking the tears away. *Isn't that something.*

She nibbled on the strawberry and thought about their earlier conversation in the basement. Was he serious? She rolled her eyes. Of course not! You don't just come out and announce to a woman that you're going to marry her and have a hundred kids. He'd had plenty of time to continue the conversation in the car, but he'd never raised the subject. A wave of disappointment washed over her. Oh, great, she thought with a grimace. Disappointment. I'm in big trouble here. My emotional clock is not in tune with The Plan.

She would have to be strong. She would refuse to fall in love—and if she was already in love she would refuse to admit it. What she needed was some good old-fashioned hostility. A mean streak to cover up all those cozy feelings.

Jake took her hand in his and tenderly kissed the inside of her wrist.

Berry snatched her hand away. "Don't kiss my wrist."

"Okay. What would you like me to kiss?"

"I don't want you to kiss anything."

"What a load of baloney." He took her hand back and kissed the soft center of her palm. His eyes sparkled mischievously. "How about if I kiss your—"

"Don't you dare!"

He sucked on the tip of her index finger. "Can I kiss it in the shower?"

"We're not taking a shower. Stop that!" She swallowed hard when he resumed the sucking, this time touching his tongue to the tip of her finger. She bopped him on the side of the head with a bag of bread. "I said stop that."

"Playing hard to get, huh?"

"I'm not playing anything. Read my lips. Get lost." Berry stood at the table. "Go home."

"I am home."

"Oh, yeah." She carted the pickle jars and packages of lunch meat to the refrigerator, feeling like the village idiot. She wasn't very good at this sort of thing. She was too inexperienced, too overwhelmed by his sexuality, too easily flustered by her own attraction to him. He made her feel like Mary Poppins with the hots.

Upstairs a door creaked open, and one of the ladies padded down the carpeted hall to the bathroom.

Jake put the last of the dishes in the dishwasher. "I'll bet you a dollar it's Mrs. Dugan. I can tell by that authoritarian thump, thump, thump of her slippers."

"Mrs. Dugan's keeping her eye on you."

"I know. She has her radar tuned to the sound of lips meeting." He pulled her into the circle of his arms. "I think we should put it to a test. Let's see how fast we can get Mrs. Dugan out of the bathroom."

She really shouldn't be kissing him, she thought, but this was sort of a scientific experiment. Who was she to stand in the way of science.

"This is the first of the good-night kisses," Jake told her. His warm lips brushed against her mouth, and his hands splayed across her lower back, pressing her gently into him. When he spoke his voice whispered into her mouth. "There are all kinds of good-night kisses. There are good-night kisses when you're done making love, and you know it's been a very special night." He kissed the sensitive spot just below her ear and moved his hand to her breast, gently cupping the soft fullness, running his thumb over the hardening peak in the middle.

"And there are good-night kisses that are the prelude to making love. Kisses that are hungry and impatient." His hand tightened slightly at her breast. His lips sought her with passionate ferocity, his tongue forcing itself deep into her mouth.

Berry heard herself moan as his arousal thrust against her, and his tongue slid erotically over hers.

The bathroom door opened and feet traversed the upstairs hallway, stopping at the head of the stairs. "Somebody down there?"

"It's just us, Mrs. Dugan," Jake answered. "We were having a bite to eat before coming to bed."

"It's late. It's time nice young ladies were in bed."

"I'm trying," Jake sighed.

"Alone!"

"Why couldn't you adopt a bunch of old ladies who were hard of hearing?"

Berry giggled. "And then there are good-night kisses that simply say 'Good night.' "

Jake watched her with eyes darkened by passion. "Not for you there aren't. There are good-night kisses that are precursors of things to come. Promises of more fulfilling encounters."

Berry took a shaky breath. "Not if Mrs. Dugan can help it."

"You're doomed, Berry." A puckish grin tugged at the corners of Jake's mouth. "So is Mrs. Dugan." He turned her towards the stairs and swatted her behind. "Go to bed."

Six

He was doing it again. He was undressed. The man was a flaming exhibitionist. Berry huddled under her covers and listened to the sounds of buttons and zippers. He had no modesty. He had no scruples. "Aren't you dressed yet?" Good grief, was that her voice? That panic-stricken squeak?

"Why don't you come out from under those covers and find out?"

Berry didn't have to come out from under the covers. She knew he wasn't dressed. She could tell by the goose bumps on her arm. Damn him, anyway. "Why do you have to get dressed in my room?"

"Because this is my room, too. Because this is where my clothes are. Because there are little old ladies occupying both bathrooms, and I'm in a hurry this morning. Because I get my kicks this way, and with Mrs. Dugan around kicks are hard to come by—you have to take them when you can." He pulled the covers back and kissed her on the nose. "You should have looked. It would have been a lot more fun."

He was wearing grey slacks, and a red-and-white pin-striped shirt. Berry watched him move to his closet and select a tie from a well-stocked rack. "Did you really want me to look?"

"Uh-huh."

"You would have been the only one undressed. Wouldn't you have been embarrassed?"

"Yeah. That's the fun part. You know what happens when men get embarrassed? They get—"

"I know what they get. And you'd better not!"

He gave his tie a small tug and turned to face her. "What do you think? Do I look like a first-grade teacher?"

Berry thought he looked more like a fully clothed model for a Chippendale's calendar. She sat up in bed and told her heart to stop jumping around like that. He was just a man, for goodness' sake. An ordinary man wearing a pair of pants that were perfectly tailored across his slim hips and nifty butt. An ordinary man wearing a shirt that was exquisitely cut to fit luscious broad shoulders and a just-right muscled chest that tapered down to a hard flat stomach. Why on earth was she getting so tense over this ordinary man?

Because he wasn't ordinary. He was totally delicious and she should have looked. She was a fool not to have looked. After all, she had already seen almost all of him. There was only about five or six inches left to her imagination. The memory of those six inches could probably have carried her through old age. She swallowed and stared at him in her best attempt at unblinking serenity. "You look very nice. Any first grader would be proud to have you for a teacher."

"Thank you," he bowed slightly. "I have to run. I've called the rental agency. They're sending a car around for you to use. Should be here by eight o'clock." A cab beeped in the driveway. Jake took keys and loose change from the bureau top and grabbed a camel-hair blazer from the closet.

Berry listened to him bound down the stairs and out the door. She sprang from her bed and rushed to her window for one last glimpse of him as he climbed into the cab. Too late. He was gone. He was dressed. "Dammit," she whispered, "I really should have looked."

She was still thinking about it at the breakfast table when she noticed an unusual silence. Everyone was watching her. "Sometning wrong?"

"No."

"Nothing?"

"Uh-uh. Nothing wrong with me."

Berry looked at the clean teacups and unused cereal bowls. "Not eating?"

"Maybe later."

"In a minute."

"Not just yet."

"Not even tea?" Berry asked.

Mrs. Fitz fidgeted in her seat. "Well, we brewed some. We just haven't gotten around to drinking it yet."

Berry poured herself a bowl of cereal and reached for the milk. She stopped short. "Oh."

"Something wrong, dear?"

"No. Of course not." She stared at the milk carton. She stared at the cereal. It looked like raisin bran. She gently pushed the raisins around with the tip of her finger. She raised her eyes to the three women. "Looks like raisin bran."

"Yes."

"I thought so, too."

"Uh-huh."

Berry sniffed at the bowl. "Smells like raisin bran."

"Does it?"

"That's good."

Mrs. Fitz narrowed her eyes. "Okay, pour the milk in."

Berry pushed the bowl over to her. "*You* pour the milk in."

Mrs. Fitz pushed the bowl back. "Not me. No way. No, sir. Took me half an hour to get the cereal out of my hair yesterday."

Berry compressed her lips. "This is ridiculous. This is just plain old raisin bran." She moved her seat back a few inches and dribbled some milk into her bowl. Nothing happened.

"Stir it," Mrs. Fitz suggested.

Berry stirred it. It didn't crackle or pop. It didn't fly out into space. It didn't even bloat. "Raisin bran."

Mrs. Fitz filled her bowl. "Thank the Lord, I'm so hungry I could eat a horse."

Mildred served tea, and all three women sipped timidly.

"Tastes like tea," Mildred offered.

Mrs. Dugan agreed.

Mrs. Fitz swallowed a spoonful of cereal. "Don't know whether I'm relieved or disappointed, but I'll tell you one thing. Tomorrow morning I'm getting up in time to have breakfast with Jake. From now on he eats everything first."

Berry ladled a generous helping of tomato sauce onto a pizza round and covered it with mozzarella. She drizzled a smidgen of olive oil across the masterpiece and looked up as the front door swung open and Jake sidled through carrying two grocery bags. He was followed by an elderly man, also carrying a grocery bag. From the corner of her eye

Berry saw Mrs. Fitz wipe her hands on her apron and pat a stray hair into place.

"Bandit at six o'clock," Mrs. Fitz whispered, "I'm going in for the kill."

"Mrs. Fitz, you've been watching too much television."

"Movies. Namely, *Top Gun*. Isn't that Tom Cruise a honey?"

Jake set the bags on the counter and extracted four plastic cartons containing salad. "Where's Mildred and Mrs. Dugan?"

"Their night off."

Jake pulled a stool up to the counter. "Here you go, Harry. We're missing two ladies. Guess you'll have to eat lots of salad." Jake made a sweeping gesture with his hand. "Berry and Mrs. Fitz, I'd like you to meet my good friend, Harry Fee."

Mrs. Fitz held out her plump hand. "My name's Lena. Here's a fork. You want to go to the movies later?"

Berry raised her eyebrows at Jake. "I'd like to see you back by the refrigerator, please."

Jake brought a bag with him and haphazardly transferred food from the bag to the refrigerator.

"What do you think you're doing?" Berry whispered.

"Putting the food away."

"I don't mean about the food. Wait a minute, why are you putting all this food in here? Yogurt? Oranges? Is this tuna salad?"

"You never eat anything. When the ladies were upstairs they made you come up for supper. Now that they're at my house you make do with candy bars."

"Who told you that?"

"I have my sources."

"It's lie. I take good care of myself . . . most of the time."

"Nobody could take care of herself with the schedule you're running. You're suffering from too little time and too little money. You study for school while you roll out pizza dough, and you're wearing running shoes that are held together with surgical tape because you're trying to save money to buy a new jeep. If that isn't enough, you constantly let your heart rule your head. The ladies are lovely people, but they require naps, they can't drive, they can't deliver." He paused and longingly looked at Berry's mouth. "They can't kiss."

"Of course they can kiss, and how did we get to talking about kissing, anyway?"

He nibbled on her left earlobe. "You have this erotic effect on me." He kissed the pulse point in her neck. "It's become an obsession. All I ever think about is kissing you. Well, that's not totally honest . . . I think about doing other things to you, too, but they're related to kissing."

"Get serious."

His knee nudged against the inside of her thigh. "I'm trying. You're not cooperating."

Berry tried to concentrate, but for the life of her she couldn't remember why they were back there, standing against the refrigerator. It might have something to do with tuna salad. No, she thought, that's not it.

Mrs. Fitz bustled around the front of the store. She gave Harry Fee a coke and a hot piece of pizza. "We'll have to go to the late show," she told Harry. "I have to help Berry until the place closes."

Jake nuzzled Berry's hair and molded his hand to her hip. "That's okay, Mrs. Fitz, I'll help Berry tonight."

Berry wriggled away. "No!"

"Yes." Jake was firm.

"You helped me last night and the stupid car

got stolen. I don't want your help. You're nothing but a pain in the neck."

Jake put his arm around her and kissed the top of her head. "She's crazy about me," he told Harry. "But she's shy. You know how women are. . . ."

Mrs. Fitz got her sweater and her purse. "She's a ninny," she mumbled to Harry. "Don't know opportunity when it comes knocking."

Harry's blue eyes twinkled. "I bet you don't pass up any opportunities, Lena."

"Not if I can help it. Trouble is, opportunities don't come along often enough."

Harry held the door for her and winked at Jake. "Don't wait up."

Berry's mouth fell open. "What did he mean by that?"

"He meant they're going to have an enjoyable evening at the movies, and we shouldn't wait up."

"That dirty old man has designs on Mrs. Fitz," Berry shrieked.

"I don't believe this. You're doing a Mrs. Dugan."

"If anything happens to that dear, sweet old lady, I'm holding you personally responsible."

"Are you kidding me? I'm worried about Harry."

Berry took several pizzas from the oven and shoveled them into boxes. "Is he a really good friend? How long have you known him?"

Jake looked at his watch. "Forty-five minutes."

"What?"

"I met him in the supermarket. Actually, I had him lined up for Mrs. Dugan. Guess I'll have to go back to prowling the frozen food section tomorrow. Frozen food is a good place to meet old guys."

"You . . . you purveyor!" she sputtered, wide-eyed and furious. "I know what you're up to. I'm not stupid. You're getting rid of my ladies. You're getting them out of the house so you can talk about soap!"

"Yup."

"You admit it?"

"Yup."

"That's despicable."

He slouched casually against the counter, hands in his pockets. "Mrs. Fitz and Mrs. Dugan and Mildred are three terrific ladies. They're bright and lively—and lonely. It doesn't take a genius to figure out that they'd like some male companionship once in awhile. And it doesn't take a genius to figure out that I'd have to be Houdini to get you into bed with Mrs. Dugan around. I think I've reached a very creative solution to everyone's problem."

Berry clenched her fists. "Not my problem. My problem is getting rid of you. You're ruining my plan. I don't want a relationship. I don't want your tuna salad. I was doing just fine until you came along. For the first time in my life I knew where I was going. I had goals, direction, purpose. I had self-esteem." She clenched her fists in vexation. "Now I don't know what I have. Now I have hot flashes and uncomfortable cravings."

Jake looked outrageously pleased at that. "Really?"

"I don't need uncomfortable cravings. I need to study my art history. You can understand that, can't you?" Berry pleaded.

Jake took a step towards her. "What sort of cravings?"

"None of your business."

"Ah, but it is my business." His voice was soft and pleasantly raspy, and he stood so close Berry could feel the warmth from his body swirl around her. "I feel an obligation to take care of these uncomfortable cravings."

He didn't understand, Berry thought sadly. She

had plenty of the type of cravings he was referring to, but they weren't the ones that scared her. It was the pudding cravings, and the baby cravings, that turned her stomach into a churning turmoil. It was the way she felt when she did his laundry and found herself fondling his clean white sweat socks, worrying if they were soft enough, white enough.

"Wouldn't you like to tell me about these cravings?" he teased silkily.

"No. Never."

"Guess I'll have to resort to torture to wring the truth from you. You'll like my torture," he grinned.

Berry was speechless. She stared at him, totally nonplussed, unable to decide how she felt about any of this. She wasn't sure if Jake was a cad or a hero, but she was sure of one thing—he had a smile that was half little boy, half pirate, and one hundred percent effective.

She decided to ignore it and go with a safer subject. "Is this my salad?"

Jake chuckled and pushed the salad towards her. "You can run, but you can't hide, especially since you're living in my house."

Berry munched a slice of carrot. "Tomorrow my apartment gets painted. Next they install carpet. I intend to run like hell for the rest of the week and then hide in my own safe little apartment until the only cravings I have left are for pizza and art history."

"Hmmm."

Berry paused with her fork in midair. That was such a sneaky 'hmmm.' It wasn't discouraged or disconsolate. It wasn't even apprehensive. It was smug. Frighteningly smug.

• • •

Rain slashed down the plate-glass windows of the Pizza Place, casting the small shop in funeral shadow. The ovens were warm against Berry's back, but the fluorescent lighting did nothing to dispel the gloom of cold April showers.

The front door swung open and two bedraggled men entered, stomping the rain off their sneakered feet. Their first reaction was to sniff the air and smile appreciatively.

"Lady, if I were you, I'd move my bed down here. The pizza smells great."

Berry handed them each a slice on a paper plate. "Are you done? Is my carpet all installed?"

"Yeah. Boy, I was never so glad to be done with a job in my life. Nothing personal, but your apartment really stinks."

Berry felt her cheeks color with embarrassment. "There was a fire. And it's just been painted."

"What kind of paint did you use? That place smells like old socks."

The second man shook his head. "Worse than old socks . . . that place smells like dead socks."

Berry looked at Mildred and Mrs. Fitz. "Maybe I'd better go investigate." She and Jake had checked on it this morning, and it had definitely had a strong paint odor. She hadn't been able to open the windows because of the rain, but she'd assumed the fumes would have dissipated by now. When she reached the top of the stairs her eyes began to sting. Paint, new carpet, dead socks. They were right. It smelled bad, really bad. Worse than this morning. The walls were eggshell white, and the insurance had paid for not the best but not the worst grade of beige wall-to-wall carpet. The windows were sparkling clean. There was insurance money for new curtains and a new couch but no time to shop for them.

She turned at the sound of footsteps on the stairs and smiled at Jake before he pulled her to him and kissed her hello. Just as he always did. As if they belonged to each other, she thought. Casual husbandly kisses. Hello, good night, good morning. There had been no more invitations to share a shower. No more forays under her pajama top. It should have been a relief, but it wasn't—it was driving her crazy.

Jake wrinkled his nose. "What's that smell?"

"It's my apartment," she moaned. "How am I going to live in this?"

"Don't worry. It's probably just a combination of fresh paint and new carpet. It'll be better in a few days."

Berry felt like screaming. In a few days she'd be a babbling, drooling idiot. She needed to get away from Jake Sawyer. She needed to get out of his bed, out of his house, away from his shower. Especially his shower. A morning shower used to be a wake-up ritual. Now it was an erotic experience that brought her to the breakfast table cracking her knuckles.

Jake looked down at her. "You have a peculiar expression on your face. Sort of desperate."

Desperate. The perfect word. She turned from him so he wouldn't see the fib. "Not desperate. Just disappointed. I'd hoped to move in tonight."

"Obviously that's out of the question. Looks like you're destined to stay with me a little longer," he said cheerfully.

"Maybe it'll smell better tomorrow."

"I doubt it. Not if it keeps raining, and you can't open the windows."

"You seem awfully pleased about all of this."

"I like having you in my bed."

Berry was sure her heart stopped beating. It

went *thud* and then she felt nothing. Nothing but tingles in every erotic body part she owned. The truth was, she liked being in his bed. She liked imagining him next to her, his arm possessively curled across her chest, his lips pressed against her shoulder . . . Good grief, what was she doing, drifting off into fantasyland. It must be the fumes, making her stupid. "You make it sound like a group activity."

"I fantasize a lot. Don't you?"

"Never. Absolutely never. And stop grinning like that."

"Sometimes you're such a goose." He draped his arm around her and ushered her down the stairs. "So, how are you and Mrs. Dugan doing today? Selling lots of pizzas?"

"Mrs. Dugan isn't working today. Mildred's working today."

He stopped and grasped her shoulders. "Are you putting me on? I asked Mrs. Dugan at the breakfast table, and she said this was her shift."

"She decided to trade with Mildred. It had to do with, uh, irregularity, I think."

"How could she possibly have irregularity? We've got stewed prunes, prune juice, dried prunes, and bran nuggets."

"I'm afraid to ask why you're so concerned about Mrs. Dugan's work schedule."

Jake removed his slicker and wrapped it around her shoulders. He opened the downstairs door and gave Berry a push into the rain. "Run for it."

Mildred didn't bother to look up when Berry and Jake burst into the store. She was instructing a burly elderly gentleman in the art of pizza making. "My goodness, you're good at this," she murmured to him.

"Used to be a cook in the navy. And then when

my hitch was done I was a butcher. Ran my own shop for forty years, until I retired seven years ago." He shook his head. "Should never have retired. Life is damn boring. The wife and I were going to travel, but she died before we did much of anything."

"I'm sorry," Mildred whispered.

He made a dismissive gesture with his hand. "It's okay. We had a good life together."

Berry glared at Jake. "You've done it again."

"He was supposed to be for Mrs. Dugan."

"You were going to fix Mrs. Dugan up with a man who has a tattoo on his arm?"

Jake grinned. "It's an anchor."

Mildred slid the pizza into an oven and waved to Berry. "This is William Kozinski. I was showing him how to make pizza."

William Kozinski extended his hand. "Bill. I'm Jake's friend."

Berry looked at him through slitted eyes. "Of course you are."

"Everyone wants pizza delivered tonight," Mildred said. "No one wants to go out in the rain."

Jake balanced the boxes in his arms. "Come on, Berry. You drive. I'll deliver."

Berry looked around. "Where's Mrs. Fitz?"

"She just left." Mildred beamed. "She had a date!"

Bill held up his large butcher's hand. "Don't worry about a thing. Mildred and I can handle things here. You young folks go off and do your deliveries."

Berry turned to Jake. "I'm not leaving this geriatric Lothario alone with my cash register," she whispered angrily.

"He's my sister's father-in-law."

"Oh."

Berry slid behind the wheel and turned the key. Rain buffeted the car and dark clouds roiled overhead. "Where's the first delivery?"

"Sudley Road."

Berry faced him. "Sudly Road? That's pretty far away. Don't we have anything closer?"

"Nope."

Another one of those nights, she sighed. It was hard to make money when she was driving all over the county. In fact, the profit on these nighttime deliveries was marginal once she surpassed a three-mile radius. Heat from the pizzas drifted forward, warming Berry's neck, and the cozy aroma of fresh-baked dough filled the car.

Jake relaxed in the seat next to her, content with his role of riding shotgun. Berry watched him from the corner of her eye and thought that sometimes life was very comfortable with Jake. There wasn't the need to fill every moment with chatter. In fact, if she had to analyze her feelings for him, she would have to admit to feeling— married. It was especially disconcerting since she had been legally married to Allen for four years and never once felt this companionable affection. Life was strange, and there was no accounting for emotions. Emotions went their own way willy-nilly, without consulting The Plan.

Jake sat up straighter as they turned onto Sudley and checked the house numbers. "The white ranch on the left." He grabbed the pizza box and splashed his way to the front door. By the time he got back he was soaked.

Berry grimaced at the sight of his ruined loafers. She should never have let him do the deliveries. He wouldn't accept any pay. Not even tips. Yet every day he came directly from school and worked at the Pizza Place until closing. The fact that she was beginning to rely on his help only compounded her feelings of guilt.

After the third delivery he didn't bother with the hood to his jacket. He couldn't get any wetter. After the seventh pizza he took his shoes off and rolled his pants to midcalf. It was six o'clock and getting dark.

"That's it," he announced, squishing into the car. "I'm going home. I'm not delivering any more pizzas."

Berry looked in the back seat. "We have one last delivery."

"Too bad. Let them eat cereal. I'm cold and I'm wet and this whole thing is stupid. You're not even making any money on these deliveries."

"But I always deliver—"

"Not any more you don't. We're going home to talk."

"Just what are we going to talk about?"

"We're going to talk about this pizza business. Then we're going to talk about us."

"There's nothing to discuss. My pizza business is doing fine, and there's no us. What we have is a living arrangement which will soon be terminated. I don't mean to sound ungrateful. You've been very kind—"

"Kind?" he shouted. "You think I'm kind?"

"Well, yes."

"I've been kind to your three old ladies, but I haven't been kind to you."

"What have you been?"

"Waiting, mostly. Trying to get rid of Mrs. Dugan. I can't get ten minutes alone with you. The only time we're alone is when we're delivering pizzas, and then I'm busy with my nose in a map or you're falling asleep on the seat beside me. Your lifestyle is not conducive to romance."

"I know that, Sherlock." Berry turned into

Ellenburg Drive. "I've told you before. I don't have time for romance."

"Wrong. You don't want to have time for romance."

"What's that supposed to mean?"

"It means you're still running scared from your first marriage." His finger lightly stroked her cheek. "Let it go, Berry. Give yourself a chance to fall in love again."

"You don't understand. I have goals."

"You make falling in love sound like a terminal illness."

Berry pulled into the garage and cut the ignition. "I feel guilty about this last pizza."

"I don't. I'm sure the people who ordered it have already eaten something else. It took us almost two hours to deliver seven pizzas in this damn rain. Let's heat it up in the microwave and eat it." He opened the kitchen door for Berry and set the pizza on the counter. "I'll be right back. I'm going to take a hot shower and change my clothes."

Berry paced in the kitchen. Jake was wrong. She didn't make herself busy just to avoid romance. Did she? Of course not. But if she did, it was for good reason. She had priorities. She had a plan. Damn that plan. She was beginning to hate it, and it was all Jake's fault. He made her dissatisfied. He dangled all sorts of forbidden pleasures under her nose. For crying out loud, she'd had a hard enough time doing without butterscotch pudding—now she had romance added to her list.

She heard the water stop running in the upstairs bathroom. Jake was done with his shower. She popped the pizza into the microwave and hastily scribbled a note telling Jake she'd gone back to the Pizza Place to help Mildred. Was she running away from romance? Darn right she was.

• • •

Berry entered the darkened kitchen on tiptoe. It was twelve o'clock, and if she had any luck at all, no one would wake up. She inched across the floor, waiting for her eyes to adjust to the dim light, and almost screamed out loud when she stumbled into Jake.

His voice was soft and lethally lazy. "It's late."

Berry used to go fishing with her Uncle Joe back in McMinneville. They'd sit all day in the warm shade of a willow tree, listening to the hypnotic drone of dragonflies and crickets, and then when she was just about asleep, Uncle Joe's voice would buzz low in her ear. "Well, look at this . . . big ol' catfish is finally taking my bait. If we just wait here nice and quiet that fish'll hook himself . . . and we'll have catfish for dinner." That was the sort of voice Jake had used. A catfish-catching voice.

Berry made an effort to swallow the panic that was rising in her chest. "Mildred and Bill left early, and I stayed around to tidy up."

His hands were at her neck, massaging little circles. "You feel tense."

You bet I'm tense, she thought. I'm not as dumb as that ol' catfish. I know when I'm about to become dinner.

She felt his breath whisper through her hair while his hands slid over her shoulders and nestled against the fullness of her breasts. It was an act of gentle possession. As was the taking of her mouth: a silent affirmation of the power he held over her. His tongue touched hers in confident intimacy, and she felt his arousal stir against her belly. She placed both hands against his chest and pushed away. "Lord, you're probably murder on catfish, too."

Even in the dark she could see the look of astonishment on his face. "Catfish?" He rested his head against the refrigerator and groaned. "Do you hear someone at the front door?"

"Mildred?"

The door opened and Bill's voice drifted through the dark house in a stage whisper. "Mildred, I had a great time tonight."

Mildred's answer was low and indiscernable. There was a prolonged silence.

"Holy smoke," Berry said, "you don't suppose they're . . ."

"Sounds to me like he's got a more cooperative partner than I do, the old coot."

Berry and Jake cringed at the unmistakable thump, thump, thump of Mrs. Dugan thundering down the hall, stomping down the stairs. A light flashed on in the living room.

"Mmmmmmmildred!" Mrs. Dugan pronounced it like a drum roll.

"This is Bill Kozinski. We were just saying good night."

"He has a tattoo."

"It's an anchor. He was in the navy."

A car door slammed in the driveway and Mrs. Fitz and Harry joined the party.

"What the devil is this?" Mrs. Fitz demanded. "Why isn't everyone asleep?"

Mrs. Dugan stood her ground. "You'd like that. You'd like to have the living room all to yourself, I suppose."

"Darn right. How're we supposed to neck with you standing there gawking at us?"

Bill put his arm around Harry's shoulders. "Time to leave." They made a quick exit.

Mrs. Fitz glared at Mrs. Dugan. "See what you've done. You make them go away."

Mrs. Dugan shook her finger at Mrs. Fitz. "You'll never catch a man that way. Everyone knows men don't buy what they can get for free."

"Well, that's fine with me 'cause I don't want to be bought."

"Me either." Mildred giggled. "I don't want to be bought, but I might be persuaded to give it away for free."

Mrs. Dugan and Mrs. Fitz instantly turned scarlet. "Mildred!"

"I think we should all go into the kitchen and make a nice pot of tea." Mildred smiled pleasantly. "I'm just dying to tell someone about Bill."

Jake groaned. "What did I do to deserve this?"

Seven

Berry sipped her orange juice and watched Jake from the corner of her eye. He was clearly lost in his own thoughts. He glanced at the clock while he unconsciously drank his coffee. An air of brooding expectancy gave his dark eyebrows an ominous slant, making him seem more threatening than usual. She'd successfully avoided him since the kitchen encounter, trying with little success to sort out her feelings. It was like playing the game of plucking petals off a daisy. Keep The Plan. Junk The Plan. Keep The Plan. Junk The Plan.

In the beginning it had been her body that wanted to junk The Plan, but more and more, it was her mind that wanted to love Jake Sawyer. He carried a sense of order and security with him. His life-style was a little extravagant, what with one-of-a-kind cars and exploding cereal, but his house was a home. That was the part that really scared her. Was she still looking for someone to take care of her mittens? Was she still looking for someone to fill in the blanks in her personality?

Jake Sawyer was the man every woman dreamed of, but some incomprehensible, elusive instinct gnawed at her stomach when she thought of commitment to him.

Mrs. Fitz hadn't noticed Jake's preoccupation. She was contemplating the raspberry-colored egg on her breakfast plate. "Looks like Jell-O. Is it Jell-O?"

Jake checked the clock one more time. "Nope. It's not Jell-O."

Mrs. Fitz tried to cut it, but it skittered across the table. "Slippery little devil," she remarked.

Berry had a similar object on her plate. It was green. "You sure this is edible?"

Jake looked injured. "Of course it's edible. It's also entirely natural and high in protein."

"How'd it get green?"

"Spinach extract."

Berry rolled it onto her spoon and watched in dismay as it slithered off slinky style. "How do you eat it?"

Jake leaned back in his chair. "That's the fun part."

"You have a bizarre idea of fun."

Mrs. Fitz poked it with her finger. "Is this a bedroom toy? Is this for those people who spray themselves with whipped cream?"

Mrs. Dugan looked up horrified. "Land sakes, Lena. You're such a pervert. Where do you get these ideas?"

"Well, it don't seem right for breakfast," Mrs. Fitz complained. "At seven o'clock in the morning I don't have the energy to chase my food around."

Mildred glanced at her watch. "It's not seven o'clock. It's nine-thirty. It's Saturday."

"It don't matter. It's still too early."

Mrs. Dugan looked disdainfully at Mrs. Fitz. "If you got to bed at a reasonable time, you'd be able to get up in the morning. I think it's disgraceful, a woman your age staying out to all hours with that man."

Mrs. Fitz narrowed her eyes at Mrs. Dugan. "What do you mean a woman my age? I'm not so old. Besides, I'm getting younger now that I have a beau. Haven't had this much fun in twenty years."

Mildred looked happily pensive as she stirred her tea. "I think I'm in love," she sighed.

Mrs. Fitz shook her head. "It's the quiet ones that fool you. Three dates, and she's gooney-eyed."

"Isn't this something," Mildred said. "Just like the Love Boat where everyone falls in love. Lena and Harry, me and Bill, Berry and Jake—"

"Berry and Jake are not in love," Berry shouted.

Jake raised his eyebrows.

Mrs. Fitz looked disgusted. "Of course you're in love. Any ninny could see you're in love."

Berry gritted her teeth and busied herself with her green egg. She held it firmly in her hand and tried to stab it with her fork. "I'm not in love, and Jake certainly isn't in love," she said.

Jake looked at her with amused curiosity. "How do you know I'm not in love?"

"It takes a long time to fall in love. We hardly know each other."

Jake grinned suggestively. "I think I know you pretty well."

Berry felt the blush rise from her shirt collar. If he elaborated on that she'd hit him with her slimy green egg.

Mrs. Dugan sniffled and stared at her fingernails.

"Oh, dear," Mildred said, "I think one of us missed the Love Boat."

Mrs. Fitz put her arm around Mrs. Dugan's shoulders. "Don't worry, Sarah, Jake'll find a man for you."

Mrs. Dugan stiffened her spine. "I don't need Jake to find me a man. If I wanted a man I'd find one myself. It doesn't bother me that I'm the only one here without a boyfriend. Doesn't bother me at all."

Jake folded his hands behind his head and tipped back in his chair, looking totally pleased with himself. In fact, Berry thought, he looked downright triumphant.

Everyone jumped when the doorbell rang.

"My word," Mrs. Fitz said, "that's the first time someone's come to the door since we moved in here."

Jake smiled and stood. "Probably just the paper boy collecting."

The four women watched while Jake opened the front door wide to reveal a young man from a courier service. Jake took an envelope from the messenger and waved it at Mrs. Dugan. "It's for you."

Mrs. Dugan covered her mouth with her hand. "Someone's died."

Jake placed the envelope on the table. "I don't think so. The return address is from a travel agency."

Mrs. Dugan still looked worried when she opened it. She scanned the letter and her eyes opened wide. "I don't understand this. This must be one of those advertising gimmicks."

Mrs. Fitz snatched the letter from Mrs. Dugan. "Lord, we're all sitting here dying of curiosity." Her lips moved while she read. "Sarah, you've won a trip on a cruise ship!"

Berry pressed her lips together and scowled at Jake. "Cruise ship?"

Jake smiled innocently. "Looks like the Love Boat's going to sail for Mrs. Dugan, after all."

Mrs. Fitz continued reading. "It says here this

travel agency is running a senior citizens' singles cruise, and your name was drawn to get a free ticket. All expenses paid. This is real, Sarah. I know about these cruises. They're wonderful. Dottie Silverstein went on one last year."

Mrs. Dugan fidgeted with her teacup. "I don't know. I'll have to think about this. A singles cruise. Goodness."

"You better make up your mind fast. This boat sails tomorrow," Mrs. Fitz told her.

Mrs. Dugan looked at the color brochure that accompanied the letter. "The boat does look pretty. I've never been on a big boat before."

Mrs. Fitz slapped her leg. "Ain't this something? You live long enough and you get to do just about everything."

Mrs. Dugan stood at her seat. "I'll do it!" She placed her hand over her heart. "I have to tell you, I'm scared to death."

Berry looked at the brochure and mentally reviewed Mrs. Dugan's wardrobe. She would need evening clothes, a bathing suit, a few casual outfits—none of which were hanging in her closet. The women had been getting by with a bare minimum for years. Their clothes consisted of a few practical dresses and well-worn sweaters. "I'm going to get another cup of coffee," Berry mumbled.

She took her cup into the kitchen and quietly emptied the sugar bowl she'd been using as a piggy bank. She'd been saving money for a jeep, but this was an important emergency. She suspected Jake was behind this free ticket and that his motives weren't entirely honorable, but it didn't matter right now. Mrs. Dugan had an opportunity to do something special. She counted the money lying on the counter. Almost three hundred dollars. It wasn't a huge amount, but Mrs.

Dugan would be able to buy a few pretty things with it.

Berry bowed low in front of Mrs. Dugan and presented her with the cash. "I hereby bestow upon you a paltry sum of money for the purpose of decking yourself out in grand style for this romantic cruise." Berry turned to Mrs. Fitz and Mildred. "Ladies, you're excused from pizza-making for the day. I expect you to chaperon Mrs. Dugan on her rounds of the stores. Don't let her pick up any cute young salesmen—she has to save herself for this cruise."

Mrs. Dugan blushed and smiled. "Well, I might pick up one or two . . . just for practice."

Berry felt the laughter bubbling in her throat. Was this stuffy old Mrs. Dugan talking?

Mrs. Dugan hugged Berry. "I know this is jeep money, and I promise I'll pay it all back. I'll work twice as hard when I come back."

The tears were hot behind Berry's eyes. Mrs. Dugan was suddenly so much younger and happier. It was as if she was a sponge—all dry and shriveled one minute, and then suddenly swelling into radiant plumpness with the promise of a romantic adventure. Why hadn't she seen this? Why hadn't she realized Mrs. Dugan simply needed to have some fun? The answer took her breath away. She'd been so busy depriving herself of fun that she'd accepted Mrs. Dugan's stern stoicism as natural. Lord, was that true? Berry rubbed her forehead with her fingertips. Maybe she'd gotten carried away with her goals. Maybe it wasn't healthy to totally eliminate butterscotch pudding from your life.

At seven o'clock Berry turned the sign in the window to read CLOSED.

Jake looked up from the cash register. "Something wrong?"

"We're closing early tonight. We're having a bon voyage party."

Jake put his hand to her forehead. "You running a fever?"

Berry threw her baker's apron on the counter. "Not yet, but the night is still young."

"I like this kind of talk."

"We need party stuff. Chips and dip and cheap champagne."

"I feel like hiring a band."

"I think you've done enough already. After all, you bought Mrs. Dugan's cruise ticket."

"You don't know that for sure."

Berry locked the front door behind them. "Are you going to deny it?"

"No. But I don't think I want to admit to it, either."

"You go across the street to Groman's Bakery and see if you can get some sort of cake. Maybe you can persuade them to write something appropriate on it. I'll get the champagne and munchies and meet you back here."

Jake saluted and clicked his heels together and marched away to Groman's.

Half an hour later they rendezvoused at the car. Jake held a large white baker's box in his hands. "Wait until you see this terrific cake. Mrs. Kowalski got mad at her husband and canceled their twenty-fifth wedding anniversary party."

"And you bought their cake?"

"I got a real good deal."

Berry peeked inside. "There must be ten pounds of icing on this cake."

"Mrs. Kowalski likes icing."

Berry slid behind the wheel of the station wagon. "I'll drive, you hold the icing."

Jake settled the heavy box on his lap. "Why did you decide to do this? I was under the impression that nothing short of an invasion by aliens would get you to close the Pizza Place early."

Berry twisted her hands on the wheel. "It was the look on Mrs. Dugan's face. Like she was a little girl, and it was Christmas morning. She hadn't expected anything that nice to ever happen to her again. It made peddling pizza sort of—um—insignificant."

The hand that touched her cheek was gentle. It tangled in the hair behind her ear and caressed her neck. "You deserve nice things, too. If I gave you a cruise . . ."

"Don't even think about it. No more cruises!"

"Maybe we could go on a cruise for our honeymoon."

"HONEYMOON?" The car careened into the wrong lane and thumped against the curb, causing the cake to fly off Jake's lap, smash into the dashboard and flip over onto Jake's feet. Berry came to a screeching halt, looking first at Jake's chalk-white face and then at his brand-new loafers, buried under a mountain of icing. Berry clapped her hand over her mouth. "Oh, my god."

Jake plucked a gooey piece of cake from his trouser leg and tasted it. "Not bad."

Berry reached down and lifted a sizable lump from his cuff. "Yum, cherry filling between the layers."

"Mrs. Kowalski knows what she's doing when it comes to ordering cake."

"Ah, about the honeymoon. You did say honeymoon?"

"Mmmm. Remember my plan. Kids and dogs and a wife and stuff? Not necessarily in that order. Man, this cake is great." He offered her a piece from the dashboard. "You have to try this. One of the layers was chocolate."

"Are you serious?"

"Of course. I wouldn't kid about chocolate cake."

Berry felt her eye twitch. It had never twitched before. She thought it probably indicated a stroke coming on. "Kids and dogs and wife and stuff?"

"I told you about it in the basement the other day."

Berry had been taken for granted by the best of them, but this beat all. She clenched her teeth and peeled away from the curb. "Have you forgotten one small detail?" she rasped.

"Detail? Well, I'm not sure what kind of dogs we should have—"

"Me. What about me? What about a proposal. What about mutual agreement?"

Jake licked the cake from his finger. "If I asked you to marry me, what would you say?"

"No!"

"Exactly. I decided my best shot was to hang around and make myself lovable and indispensable."

"I . . . you . . . *ulk.*"

"How do you do that? How do you make that sort of strangled sound in your throat?"

When she stopped the car he was going to find out. She was going to place her fingers on his neck and squeeze until he made his very own strangling sounds. It would be okay. She was sure the judge would understand.

She pulled into the garage and reconsidered the choking idea. Suppose her fingers didn't choke him. Suppose they wandered over his broad shoulders and played with the baby-soft curls of hair around his ears. In the past, her fingers hadn't been too trustworthy. Probably choking was not a good idea. And what about that twinge of excitement that hit her stomach when he said honeymoon. In all honesty, before fury there had definitely been glorious delight. Better not choke him—it wasn't good taste to choke someone you might marry. Oh, lord, did she just think that?

Jake slid his feet out of his shoes. "If I'm careful I can leave most of the cake here."

Berry nodded numbly. She was doomed. So why didn't she feel doomed? Actually, she felt sort of ecstatic. A small giggle escaped before she firmly clamped her mouth shut.

Jake looked at her sidewise. "Are you laughing at me?"

"No. Honest. Absolutely not."

"I'm going to start buying my shoes by the dozen."

Berry pushed through the kitchen door and set her grocery bag on the counter.

Mrs. Fitz was making tea. "You're home early! Oh, lord, now what?" she worried. "Another fire? The Pizza Place burned to the ground?"

"I decided to close early."

"You never close early. Something happened and you don't want to tell me. Was it the gas line? Did the gas line blow up?"

Berry took a large bowl out of the cupboard and began vigorously filling it with chips. "I just closed early. Boy, you'd think I was some kind of workaholic. You'd think I never closed early before."

Mrs. Fitz gave Jake the once-over. "What happened to him?"

"Cake."

"What were you doing?" she said to Jake. "Eating it with your feet? Is this something kinky?"

"It was an accident," Berry explained. "This big cake sort of fell on him." She waved her hand in a dismissive gesture. "Anyway, we're going to have a bon voyage party for Mrs. Dugan. I even bought champagne."

Mrs. Fitz's round apple face crinkled into a smile. "What a wonderful idea. I'll go get Mildred and Sarah. They're upstairs, fussing with Sarah's new clothes."

A moment later Mrs. Dugan shyly stepped into the kitchen. "Well," she murmured, "what do you think?" She was dressed in a smart navy pantsuit with matching navy shoes and a soft white shirt. Her hair had been cut and waved into a feminine bob that was short enough to show off a pair of small pearl earrings. "I went to the beauty parlor. Do you think that was wasteful of me?"

"Mrs. Dugan, you look beautiful." Berry hugged her. "This is much more fun than buying a jeep. And the beauty parlor was a great idea."

Jake tucked a bottle of champagne under his arm and arranged five champagne glasses on a tray. "Berry, you get the snacks, and we'll have this party in the living room while Mrs. Dugan shows us her new wardrobe."

Mrs. Fitz settled herself on the couch. "Even the bathing suit. She looks pretty good for such an old bag."

"I'm not so old," Mrs. Dugan told her. "I've kept myself in shape. I'm almost as good as new."

Berry slouched low in the couch, her legs outstretched, her hand toying with her empty champagne glass. "That was nice. It would have been better if we'd had a cake, but it was still okay."

Jake slid his arm around Berry's shoulders. "The ladies are all tucked into bed for the night. I think this is a good time for us to have a serious discussion."

Silent groan. She wasn't ready for a serious discussion. A serious discussion meant a lot of questions. She knew all the questions, but she didn't know any of the answers. "Could I have another glass of champagne?"

Jake refilled her glass. "Are you sure you want more? You look a little . . . unsteady."

Berry chugged the wine and blinked when it hit her stomach. She wasn't much of a drinker. In fact, she wasn't any kind of a drinker. She was strictly root beer and orange juice—until tonight. "What d'ya mean unsteady? I'm doing very amazing at handling my liquor."

Jake grinned. "When was the last time you had a glass of champagne?"

Berry put her finger to her forehead to help herself think. "Hmmmm. It was at my cousin Melanie's wedding. We all toasted the bride, and then I threw up."

"You're not going to throw up now, are you?"

Berry shook her head. "It was food poisoning. The chicken was contanimated." She giggled. "Did I say contanimated?" She walked her fingers up Jake's shirt. "You know, you're awful cute. Sometimes I have to sit on my hands to keep from ripping your clothes off."

Jake rolled his eyes to the ceiling. "She's snockered. I finally have her alone, and she's drunk as a skunk."

"You bet I'm drunk as a skunk. Wanna take advantage of me?"

He stared at her.

"Well?" she demanded.

"I'm thinking about it."

"Heavens. What passion."

Jake sighed. "I can't do it."

"Of course you can do it. It's easy. I'll help you." She settled herself in the crook of his arm and snuggled against his chest. "First thing we have to do is get you undressed." She flipped open his top two buttons.

"Stop that! No one's getting undressed—"

"Don't be shy. I've seen you in your undress. All but a couple inches."

Jake squinted at her. "I think I've just been insulted."

"Oh." Berry giggled. "Oh, dear, you thought I meant . . . I didn't mean that couple inches. Well, I guess I did, but not in that way. Not . . . uh, extended."

"How about if I make us some coffee?"

Berry opened the last remaining button and rubbed her hand across the black velvet trickle of hair that divided his stomach. "Wow," she breathed reverently, "what a body. I must have been crazy to think you had a hunchback." She pulled his shirt aside and rested her cheek on his bare skin. "Yum," she purred, stroking the thin line of hair, "just like bread crumbs."

Jake wiped a film of sweat from his forehead. "Bread crumbs?"

"Like in Hansel and Gretel. Remember how they followed the bread crumbs to the gingerbread house?" He felt so good against her cheek, Berry thought. And the line of black hair was so enticing and so close. She could hardly resist nibbling on it. So she did. Then the nibbling progressed lower and lower until she'd trailed a line with the tip of her tongue all the way down to the waistband of his jeans. "Uh oh," she exclaimed. "Your pants are blocking the way to the gingerbread house."

"Berry!"

"Yes, Jakey?"

"I think we'd better get you up to bed."

Berry's eyes slid closed. "Not now. I'm too tired."

He pulled her to her feet, but her knees crumpled.

"Whoops," she mumbled, tumbling into him with a thud. "No knees. What happened to my knees?"

Jake scooped her into his arms and carried her to the stairs. At the third step her head bonked against the wall and her foot caught in the polished wooden railing. "Dammit," Jake swore, "this never happened to Rhett Butler."

"Who?"

He set her down on the stairs and propped her up against the wall while he contemplated the task before him. Finally, he slung her over his shoulder like a sack of potatoes and carted her off to his bedroom.

"Oh no," Berry groaned, falling spread-eagled onto the comforter, "I've got the whirlies." She draped one leg over the side of the bed until her foot touched the floor. "There, that's better."

"Honey, you can't sleep like that."

"Why not?"

"Because—"

Wump. Berry fell off the bed onto the plush carpet.

Jake bent to help her up. "That's why not."

"This is embarrassing. I've never been drunk before. I don't like it. I'm not doing this ever again. This never happens when I drink root beer."

Jake pulled back the comforter and trundled her between the sheets. He gently stroked the hair from her forehead. "Poor Berry."

"I'm okay. I'm going to sleep now."

Berry looked at Jake through half-closed eyes. "Is it always this bright in the morning?"

"How do you feel?"

"My eyes feel like two fried eggs and there are little men wearing pointy hats and spiky shoes running around in my stomach."

"Would you like some breakfast?"

"Not a chance."

Jake looked at his watch. "I'm going to have to get Mrs. Dugan to the boat. I'll drop Mrs. Fitz and Mildred off at the Pizza Place. You can take the day off."

"Mrs. Fitz and Mildred can't do deliveries."

"It's Sunday. You don't deliver on Sunday."

"Since when?"

"Since now. It's a new rule I just made up."

New rule he just made up? What a lot of nerve. Now he was making up rules for her business. She sat up in bed and roared, "Listen here, Sawyer . . ."

"Yes?"

Suddenly she didn't feel well at all. The little men in pointy hats were doing strange things in her stomach. She covered her mouth with one hand and threw the covers off with the other. "I'm going to be sick!"

She slammed the bathroom door and sank down onto the tile floor, resting her head against the porcelain tub. Ah, that was much better, she decided. Nice and cool. Now if she could just get rid of the little men in her stomach.

Jake knocked on the door. "Berry, open the door."

"I'd sooner die."

"Are you okay?"

"No, I'm not okay. I'm being sick."

"Can I help?"

"Throwing up is not a group activity."

Several minutes later she draped a wet washcloth across her forehead and opened the door. "I'm going back to bed to die, now. No deliveries on Sunday sounds like a good rule to me."

Jake helped her into bed and tucked the covers around her. "I'll be back as soon as I get rid of Mrs. Dugan."

"Don't rush. I'm just going to stay here and feel sorry for myself."

Berry poured herself a glass of cranberry juice and stood absolutely still for a moment, enjoying the quiet solitude of the kitchen. Mrs. Fitz and Mildred were at the Pizza Place, and Jake hadn't returned from the boat. Berry had slept the morning away, and then had stayed in bed for a while thinking about plans.

Plans were only guidelines, she'd decided. They were preliminary blueprints for the real project, and sometimes, even well-thought-out plans didn't work right. For instance, she was miles deep in love with Jake Sawyer years ahead of time. Why should she be so upset about that? If it turned out she could graduate several years ahead of schedule she'd be ecstatic. Why was falling in love so different?

Berry, Berry, Berry, she warned, *you're rationalizing. There is a difference.*

Oh yeah? she answered her more practical self. *Shut up.*

And then there was this business about butterscotch pudding and Mrs. Dugan. She didn't want to become a Mrs. Dugan. Now that she thought about it she realized pudding really didn't take all that long to make. Surely she could find ten minutes a week for pudding. Probably she could squeeze a little romance into her schedule, too. Of course, it would be with you-know-who . . . Mr. Yum.

She'd stretched luxuriously and licked her lips hungrily, thinking that being miserably sick had at least given her the opportunity to analyze her problems. In the calm aftermath of her first and last hangover, Berry soberly concluded that you could get carried away with deprivation and timetables.

"Down with deprivation," Berry shouted, brandishing a wooden spoon. She finished her cranberry juice and hummed happily as she hunted through the cabinets for pudding ingredients. Cornstarch, brown sugar, vanilla. She took butter and milk and eggs from the refrigerator.

Boy, she thought, life is wonderful. Here I am, happy as a clam, making pudding in my cozy kitchen. She stirred the mixture with a wire whisk while she waited for it to boil. She separated the eggs and measured the butter. Pudding from a box was okay, but it wasn't like scratch pudding. Scratch pudding was buckled shoes and Monopoly.

She was so intrigued with the thickening pudding that she almost missed the sound of the car pulling into the garage. Jake! Her heart fluttered wildly. Stop that, she commanded her heart. It's only Jake. He lives here, remember? But she couldn't stop smiling. She loved him totally, truly, passionately, ridiculously. And she wanted him.

She took the pudding off the stove and added the butter and vanilla. Yes, sir, this was a much better plan. First, make the pudding. Second, get Jake Sawyer into the sack. Third, have her head examined. She had to be crazy. Most likely it was the alcohol. It had pickled her brain. She'd heard it could do such things.

In the absence of sherbet glasses Berry poured the pudding into coffee cups. She heard Jake move to the kitchen and knew he was leaning his hip against the counter, his arms loosely crossed over his chest, watching her. She kept her eyes glued to the coffee cups, but she felt him assessing what he saw: Lingonberry Knudsen clad in a tiger-striped T-shirt and matching bikini panties. She wriggled her bare toes against the tile floor, feeling incredibly naughty and invigoratingly scared.

His voice was low and controlled and slightly smiling. "Smells great. What is it?"

"Butterscotch pudding." Was that her? All husky and inviting?

He moved across the kitchen in a movement that reminded Berry of a big cat casually stalking prey. He peered into the empty pot and scraped some pudding from the side with his finger. "It's good."

Berry lowered her fringe of curly blond lashes. "Is it?"

Their eyes locked for a moment while they exchanged a subtle look of amused understanding.

"Would you like a taste?" he asked, offering her a swipe of warm pudding on the tip of his finger.

Berry touched her tongue to his finger and watched his eyes instantly darken. She slowly licked his finger clean, running her tongue along the length of it, sucking on the tip and suggestively drawing the whole finger into her mouth. She noticed the pulse leap in his neck and felt her chest constrict at his sharp intake of breath.

"Feeling playful?" It was more of a velvet growl than an intelligible question.

Berry put the pot in the sink, took a deep breath and swallowed hard. "Actually, I feel like taking a shower . . . with lots of soap." Before turning to the stairs she made a mental note of the way his mouth dropped open. To say he was surprised at her behavior would be an understatement. That was fine, because she was surprised, too. She'd never played femme fatale before.

He made no attempt to hide his shock. "Have you been drinking again?"

"Nope. I've been doing some thinking about butterscotch pudding . . . and things." She reached the stairs and stripped off the T-shirt. The panties hit the carpet midway to the second floor. When she didn't hear footsteps behind her she turned and placed her hands on her hips. "Aren't you coming?"

"No, but I'm very close."

Berry blushed. "I didn't mean . . . oh, hell."

Jake unbuttoned his shirt as he followed her up the stairs. By the time he reached the bathroom she was already in the shower. He dropped his jeans at the bathroom door, but struggled to extricate himself from red briefs that were stretched to the breaking point.

"Awesome," Berry said, reverently.

"I think I have too much of a good thing."

"Your good thing is perfect. It's your pants that are too small."

He removed the rest of his clothing and slid the glass door open, joining her in the roomy shower stall.

He was magnificent, Berry thought. Lean and nicely muscled, his best feature nestling in a thick thatch of black curls. She realized she'd been caught staring and smiled slyly. "I finally get to see all of you."

Jake returned the smile. He took the soap from Berry's hands and worked it into a lather while his gaze slid downward, from her shoulders, to her glistening breasts and flat belly. He paused for a long moment, obviously enjoying the sight of her nakedness.

Berry waited. She knew he was going to do this

slowly, because he'd whispered the entire process in lengthy, maddeningly graphic detail on several occassions. He'd vowed to torment her with excruciating pleasures, and when the wanting became unbearable, he'd promised to prolong her delicious agony until she begged for release. The Spanish Inquisition could have used Jake Sawyer, she thought giddily.

Jake moved close enough for Berry to feel his hard arousal touch the top of her thigh. His soapy hands traveled from her neck to her shoulders and slid along the length of her arms. He lathered his hands again and cupped her small full breasts, gently kneading them with his slippery fingers, drawing slick lazy circles around the sensitive soapy areola. "Do you like when I touch you?" he asked in his sexiest voice. He teased her nipple with the tip of his finger. "Does this feel nice?"

"Yes." She could barely breathe. Nice wasn't adequate to describe the hypnotic gentle manipulations of his fingers, Berry thought dreamily. She felt his hands move from her breasts to her back. She was thoroughly soapy and completely aroused.

She took the soap from him and lathered his back, his arms, his chest. She teased his hard male nipple just as he'd teased hers, wondering at her ability to excite him, reveling in her newfound power. Her hands moved lower, across his belly, dipping into the black curls. She'd committed herself, she realized. It didn't have anything to do with delayed pleasures or rationalized rewards. She loved him and whatever they did together would be right. No wedding ceremony could ever make her feel more married than she did at this moment.

Her lips parted for his kiss, gentle at first, then

suddenly bruising when her hands wandered down to the black thatch of hair and curled around him. Her mouth opened wider as their tongues thrust against each other in a battering parody of sex that displayed the force of his passion and the strength of his control.

His soapy hands spanned her wrist and moved to her buttocks, rhythmically massaging lower and lower until his slippery fingers deftly slid into private crevices, causing her to gasp at the erotic intrusion. She blinked at him in a haze of desire, mesmerized by the strong hands that skimmed across her hips and parted her legs, tenderly exploring, seeking the exact spot where her pleasure would be most intense. "Here?" he asked hoarsely. "Do you like this?"

Berry guided his movements. She dug her fingers into his flesh and held his shoulders for support. Yes. Dear lord, yes, she liked it. This was the delicious agony he had promised, the mind-numbing ache that she didn't ever want to end, but couldn't bear a moment longer. She heard her breathing shallow and raspy. It was going to happen. She squirmed under his touch and an involuntary moan escaped from her throat as the world exploded into glittering black shards.

Jake carried her to the bed and lay beside her. He kissed her collarbone, the soft swell of breast. He kissed her stomach, the inside of each thigh. He found the swollen little mound of female delight and teased it with the tip of his tongue, reviving her hunger.

Berry writhed against him as liquid fire swirled behind her nipples and pounded between her legs. She needed him desperately. She was hot and aching to be loved, to have him moving inside her, to have him fill her with himself.

Suddenly he was covering her, his hair-rough chest moving against her sensitive breasts. Berry opened her legs to accomodate him, her eyes wide as he carefully entered her. "Berry, you're so hot and silky." He was moving slowly inside her. His eyes closed, and Berry knew he had relinquished control. His words were an urgent murmur, barely intelligible. "I love you, Berry. My god, I love you."

Berry had never known making love could be like this. She had hoped and dreamed and felt it in her heart, but she had never really known. It was more than heat and tingles and finding the spot. It was total harmony of body and soul, the desire to please and the willingness to accept pleasure at the most intensely vulnerable level. This wasn't making love . . . it was the culmination of love. It was union and everything union represented. She raised her hips to met his thrust, taking all of him, demanding more and more until they were lost in a rhythm of mindless passion.

Hours later, Berry stretched and rolled in her sleep, searching for the comfort of Jake's warmth. Now that she had allowed herself this delicious luxury, she wanted more. She wanted Jake Sawyer with a greedy hunger that she felt could never be fully quenched. She moved her naked body against his, hoping to awaken his passion. He was beautiful when aroused, she thought. Sometimes fierce and intense. Sometimes sweet and tender and touchingly gentle.

Jake drowsily opened his eyes and pulled Berry on top of him. "Mmmm," he moaned, kissing her neck, running his hand along the smooth curve of her back. "Holy cow," he exclaimed, looking at his watch, "do you know what time it is?"

Berry bravely let her hand drift down to his thigh. She didn't care about the time. She cared about Jake. She needed to feel him moving within her, calling her name. She needed to be full of him.

Jake moved out from under her and reached for his jeans. "Poor Mrs. Fitz and Mildred have been stranded at the Pizza Place all day."

Berry blinked at his sudden departure, her heart inexplicably feeling small and cold in her chest. "Do you have to go right now? Can't you stay with me for a few minutes longer?"

"No. I should have picked them up an hour ago."

Berry felt herself in the throes of a childish pout. He was right, dammit, but it didn't make her feel any less rejected. She wrapped the damp quilt around herself to hide her nudity and stomped off to the bathroom, thinking that after all these years of celibacy she could at least have picked a man who had time for her. She caught her reflection in the mirror and burst out laughing. She was being ridiculous. Sex had made her crazy.

Eight

Berry slumped deeper into the couch and furiously zapped stations with the remote control. "Twelve forty-two," she muttered, glaring at her watch. The ladies were upstairs, asleep. The cat was curled in front of the stove, asleep. Everyone was asleep but her and Jake. She'd thought it was cute when he'd had a sudden burst of inventive inspiration during supper and gone charging off down the cellar stairs. It had stopped being cute at about eleven-thirty. Now it was downright infuriating. She took a deep breath and tried to calm herself, knowing that she was being unreasonable. For the past two weeks, Jake had given up all his spare time to work in the Pizza Place. He deserved this night to himself. He was a chemist. An inventor. He needed to work at his profession. But why tonight? She moaned. How could he leave her alone like this after they'd shared such a beautiful afternoon? It was the first time she'd ever really made love with a man, and her world felt tilted. She'd expected his world would be equally tilted. "It's tilted, all right," she said, snorting.

"Tilted in the opposite direction from mine. He could hardly wait to get away from me." That was a bunch of garbage, she thought. She was letting all her old insecurities come back to haunt her. She shut the television off and crept up the stairs, telling herself that men simply looked at these things differently. They took life in stride. That was the basic difference between men and women. Women were . . . women. And men were thoughtless beasts! Berry wrenched the bedroom door open and closed it with a thunderous slam. She stripped off her clothes and flung herself into bed, covering her head with the pillow. This is just temporary insanity from too much sex, she groaned. I should have started out slowly. And I certainly shouldn't have done it the same day I made pudding. It overloaded my system. I'll feel better tomorrow.

Three hours later Berry thrashed side to side in bed. She squinted at her clock and muttered an oath. She punched the pillow and viciously kicked at the confining tangle of sheets. You were supposed to be relaxed after you made love, she fumed. You were supposed to go to sleep with a smile on your face. What was wrong with her? She'd made love all afternoon. Why wasn't she tired? Why wasn't she smiling?

Six hours later Berry half opened one eye and caught Jake tiptoeing around the room, gathering his clothes. "Jake?"

"Sorry I woke you. Go back to sleep," he whispered.

"What are you doing?" He was wearing snug tan slacks, and she stretched in catlike contentment at the sight of him with bare feet and bare chest. "Why don't you come to bed," she said, her voice soft and rumbly as a purr.

He stood over her with a tie dangling from his hand and a blue shirt thrown over his shoulder.

"I can't. I have to get to school early today. If I could just find my damn shoes . . ." He looked under the bed and grunted with satisfaction. "Found them." A quick kiss on the top of her head and he was gone.

Berry stared at the closed door and sighed. A tear formed in her eye and precariously hung on her lower lashes. She didn't want to be an alarmist, but this was beginning to feel a helluva lot like her marriage. She slipped into a pair of jeans and a soft flannel shirt and went in search of breakfast.

Mrs. Fitz was already at the round oak table, sipping tea. "Holy cow, Lingonberry, you look awful."

Berry put the water on for coffee. She clonked a coffee mug onto the kitchen counter and stared at it.

"Looks to me like you got man problems. What'd that Jake Sawyer do now?" Mrs. Fitz said.

"Nothing."

"Nothing? Uh oh. That don't sound good."

Berry propped herself up on the counter while the coffee dripped into the glass pot. "Boy, love really stinks," Berry said to the coffee pot more than to Mrs. Fitz.

"Yeah," Mrs. Fitz agreed, "it can be a bummer."

"Are you in love with Harry?"

"I don't know. It's hard to tell at my age. You don't know whether it's love or just the prune juice working."

Berry poured herself a cup of coffee and set a skillet on the stove. "You like French toast?" she asked Mrs. Fitz.

"Who's making it?"

"I am."

"Yeah. I like it."

Berry cracked three eggs into a shallow dish

and whipped them with a fork. "Good," she said, "because I'm going to make a whole loaf of it."

That night Berry parked the rental car in the driveway and solemnly stared at the house. Lights blazed from the downstairs windows and Jake's car was parked in the garage.

"Something wrong?" Mrs. Fitz asked Berry. "You've been awful quiet today."

"Tired."

"Hmmm."

"You're not going to buy that, are you?"

"Nope."

Berry hugged Mrs. Fitz. "I'm fine."

Mrs. Fitz squeezed Berry's hand. "You're all droopy because Jake didn't show up to work this afternoon. You shouldn't worry about it. He called to say he had things to do."

Berry shrugged. "I know. I'm just being silly. Boy, silly me."

Mrs. Fitz grinned. "Yeah, you're a ninny."

"Well, I may be thinking like a ninny, but I'm not going to act like a ninny." Berry pulled herself up to her full height and balanced a grocery bag on her hip. "Come on, Mrs. Fitz, let's be cheerful."

Mrs. Fitz punched her in the arm. "Good for you."

Jake was at the kitchen table when they came in. "What time is it?" he said, looking up in surprise.

"Eleven o'clock," Mrs. Fitz told him. "I'm going to bed. I'm so tired, I could sleep on nails."

When Mrs. Fitz left, Berry ran her finger along the nape of Jake's neck. She slid her arms across his collarbone and kissed him just below his earlobe. "What about you?" she asked silkily. "Are you ready for bed?"

"I'm ready to blow my brains out. Look at these workbooks." He gestured to the stacks of dog-eared notebooks spread across the table. "I'll never catch up. I didn't know I had to grade these things."

"Can't you grade them tomorrow?"

"Tomorrow I have to grade spelling workbooks." He thumped his finger on a smudged page he'd been reading. "These kids are really something. They've actually been paying attention to me. I taught them to add!"

Berry had to smile at the pride and astonishment in his voice. "Can I help?"

"No. This is something I have to do myself." He pasted a scratch-and-sniff sticker on the book and moved on to another.

Berry cracked her knuckles and sighed. She emptied the bag of groceries and polished off three butterscotch puddings. "I guess I'll go to bed," she said in a conversational tone to the kitchen.

Neither Jake nor the kitchen answered her, so she kissed Jake on the top on his head and slunk up the stairs. She didn't feel like acting cheerful anymore. She felt like acting like a ninny. She made an angry noise through clenched teeth and slammed her bedroom door. She lay back on the bed and closed her eyes, feeling the tears of frustration and disappointment trickle down her throat. There was something wrong with her, and she didn't know exactly what it was. Maybe she always chose the wrong sort of man. Maybe she expected too much.

She buried her face in her pillow and sobbed until she was exhausted, feeling like a little girl who'd waited all year for Christmas and then discovered Santa hadn't left any presents. She knew she was being foolish, but she couldn't help it. She needed some acknowledgement that something special had passed between them. She needed reassurance that Jake loved her. And she didn't want to have to beg for it.

The next morning Mrs. Fitz looked up at Berry from the breakfast table and shook her head. "Boy, I thought you looked bad yesterday, but this beats all. Your eyes look like tomatoes."

"I had a hard time getting to sleep."

"Jake didn't look so hot, either. He left about an hour ago with his hair standing on end and his tie hanging crooked."

"He say anything about me?"

"Nope. He just kept mumbling about Joey Kowalchek and how he was going to flunk math if he didn't learn how to keep his papers neater."

"Of course." Berry took a brand-new store-bought apple pie from the refrigerator, added three scoops of vanilla ice cream, and sat down across from Mrs. Fitz. "I did a lot of thinking last night. I decided I'm not going to be in love. It isn't any fun." She let a large spoonful of ice cream slide down her throat. "Eating is fun. You can count on eating."

Berry slammed the front door behind her. "That does it. Boy, that does it," she shouted, throwing her books onto the counter. She waved a piece of paper at Mrs. Fitz. "Do you know what this is? This is what being in love does to you. Makes you stupid. Makes you fail art history tests."

Mrs. Fitz put a lid on the huge jar of pizza sauce and wiped her hands on her apron. "Thought you weren't going to be in love."

"I wasn't. But I was. And now I'm not." Berry flapped her arms. "I knew this would happen. I just knew it. There's not enough room in my head to think about both Jake Sawyer and Vincent van Gogh. Ever since Jake Sawyer popped into my life

I've been neglecting my studies, and now I'm failing," she wailed. "I've worked so hard for my degree. All down the drain for a few moments of savage passion."

Mrs. Fitz's eyes opened wide. "Really? Savage passion?"

"Savage passion. The whole nine yards." Berry chomped on a bread stick. "And I'm crazy in love with him. Absolutely bonkers." She drew her eyebrows together. "But I'm not going to be. I'm going to fall out of love this instant."

"I thought you fell out of love this morning."

"Yeah, well, now I'm really out of love. I have finals coming up. If I study hard I might be able to pull my grades up." She wrapped a white apron around her waist and set her book on the counter. She was a failure at love. She couldn't afford to be a failure at art history, too.

At eleven o'clock that night Berry stared at Jake's back bent over twenty-five spelling workbooks and knew it was over. She wanted to run away, but she couldn't. She had nowhere to go.

Jake yawned and stretched. He pivoted in his chair and studied Berry. "You're very somber today."

Berry shrugged. The emptiness inside her was a constant dull throb that left her speechless. She turned and left without a word, secretly hoping he'd follow her up the stairs. He didn't. He returned to his books with a sigh and a cursory wave of his hand.

Berry removed the towel from her head, shook out her damp blond curls and rolled her eyes at the crashing, clanking sounds originating from the kitchen. Jake must have come home while she was in the shower. Only Jake could make that much noise in the kitchen.

"I can never find a damn thing in this house," Jake muttered. "Nothing's ever in the same place twice." Another volley of clattering accompanied by swearing. "Too many women! All I wanted was a pizza, and look at what I got . . . four women who can't agree where the frying pan should go."

All he wanted was a pizza! That had become painfully obvious during the past week. He hadn't said more than ten words to her since he rolled out of bed on Sunday. She stepped into a pair of lacy blue panties and tugged at her jeans, silently swearing that she was never going to bed with another man for as long as she lived. She was a flop in the sack, and she had no intention of humiliating herself ever again. She wrenched the jeans over her hips and zipped them halfway. They wouldn't zip any further. "Damn!" She stood tall and held her breath and pulled. She had them zipped, but she couldn't button the top button. A soft roll of flesh hung over the offending waistband. Berry stared at herself in the mirror. She was fat! She tapped her foot. This was all Jake's fault, the creep. She'd wanted romance, but she'd had to settle for food, and now she was *fat*. Berry gave up on the button and shrugged into a T-shirt, gaping in disbelief as it stretched taut across full breasts. Hot damn. She had cleavage. She tipped her head back and gave herself a critical look.

Jake appeared in the doorway. "Having problems?"

"My pants don't fit." She poked at the roll. "I guess this is butterscotch pudding."

"I hope this isn't going to ruin your appetite. I made a great dinner for tonight."

"You made dinner?"

"Actually, I bought it, but I made the money that paid for it."

They stopped at the entrance to the dining room and stared in silent horror.

Berry was the first to speak. "There's a dog on the table."

"Dammit, I wanted it to be a surprise."

"You succeeded." Berry looked at the empty serving bowl. "Is this bowl supposed to be empty?"

"It's supposed to be filled with beef bourguignon. That slob of a dog ate my dinner!"

"And this basket?"

"Used to be rolls in there."

Berry could hardly keep from laughing. The floppy-eared puppy resembled a furry Buddha, sitting in the middle of the table like a centerpiece. It wagged its tail against the white lace tablecloth. Thump, thump, thump. "Hard to believe this little dog could eat all that food."

"Are you kidding? Look at that stomach. She looks like a beach ball with legs."

"She ate everything but the peas."

Jake picked the dog off the table and stro' her glossy black head. "I thought she was secure in the carrier the pet store gave me."

Berry bent to retrieve a piece of ragged red cardboard. "You mean this box that's been chewed to shreds."

"Maybe we should name her Jaws." He sat her on the floor and watched her scamper in a small circle. The puppy stopped and squatted.

"Maybe we should call her Puddles."

He ran his hand through his hair. "Oh, man, look at this mess. The only name for her is Calamity Jane."

"Haven't you ever had a puppy before?"

"No. Have you?"

"No."

"It was part of my plan. You know, floppy-eared dogs running around after a pack of kids."

"Lord, you don't have a pack of kids stashed away somewhere, do you?"

Jake grinned. "No. The kids come last. They're the fun part. We get to make the kids."

"We?"

"Oh, no! Oh damn! Your dog just threw up on my foot."

"*My* dog? Oh, no," she said, making no attempt to hide her pleasure.

"This never happens in the movies. You ever see a dog throw up on Robert Redford's foot when he's trying to be romantic?"

Berry looked at him suspiciously. "Why are you trying to be romantic?"

"It's the weekend. I'm finally caught up with my school work, and I thought we could get . . . reacquainted."

"Reacquainted?" She felt the anger boiling in her veins and took a deep breath. She'd cried for an entire week and eaten herself into blimpdom and now he wanted to get reacquainted. Now he was talking about dogs and kids. Well, she didn't need that kind of a husband. Lord, what an insensitive clod.

"It's been really nice of you to be so understanding," he said, running his hand through his hair. "You can't imagine what it's been like for me to have to sit here grading papers until all hours of the morning. Sometimes I just felt like walking away from it all and climbing into bed with you, but I couldn't do that to those kids."

Berry felt the blush rising from her shirt collar. "Um, no, you couldn't do that to the kids," she said meekly.

"Now that I'm caught up, I wanted to do something special for you. A romantic dinner for two, some very private dancing, and some very passionate lovemaking."

Berry didn't know what to think. She felt like a heel for being jealous of twenty-five first graders, but she couldn't shake the feeling of failure and rejection. "Why don't you go upstairs and wash up while I take care of this mess."

When Berry had the floor completely clean she tucked the puppy under her arm and carried her to a grassy knoll overlooking the little stream. A week ago everything had been bleak and brown, but April rains and unusually warm weather had prompted grass to grow and trees to bud. Berry stretched flat on her stomach and smiled. Calamity Jane bounded down a grassy slope, yelped in fright when she confronted a dandelion, and raced back. Berry hugged the little dog. "Would you like to know a secret?" she whispered. "I've always wanted a little black dog with floppy ears."

The puppy looked like she might explode with happiness. She furiously wagged her tail and rolled on her back. When she spied Jake coming out of the house she rushed up the hill to greet him.

Jake set a cardboard box on the ground and spread a snow-white linen tablecloth next to it. "The alternate plan for the evening is an exotic, romantic picnic." He placed two crystal goblets on the table cloth.

Berry skeptically looked at the bottle in his hand. "Champagne?"

"No. I decided to play it safe and go with sparkling apple cider." He added two sterling silver candlestick holders with lavender tapers, lavender linen napkins, two white-and-gold china plates and a silver tray laden with elaborately decorated petits fours. He plunked a foil-wrapped package on each of the Lenox plates. "Peanut butter and jelly," he explained. "My speciality."

"Good. I love peanut butter and jelly."

Jake lit the candles and leaned back on one

elbow to watch the sun settle into the trees. Brilliant shades of orange and pink flamed on the horizon and then gave way to gentle night tones of mauve and shady green as the sun sank lower. A soft breeze played over the hillside. The candles flickered and tiny tree frogs sang evening songs along the wooded banks of the creek.

Berry wiggled her bare toes in the grass. "This is better than beef bourguignon. This is perfect." She studied Jake and secretly concluded he was the most perfect of all. His feet were bare, his long legs encased in clean faded jeans that subtly displayed lean, powerful muscles and hinted at barely checked virility. The blue rugby shirt casually draped over delicious broad shoulders accented the strong column of his neck. His eyes seemed smokey in the half light, hiding his thoughts.

Berry hoped her thoughts were just as well hidden. They were a confusing, painful mixture of hope and dispair, love and anger, guilt and pride. Last Sunday she'd been so overwhelmed with love that she'd wanted to merge forever, body and soul, with Jake Sawyer. That had been wrong. You can't give up your identity and your goals in the name of love, she thought. It placed too heavy a burden on the other person. Successful relationships found a balance. That was the hard part, finding the balance. She had no confidence in being able to do that.

The little dog curled up on a corner of the tablecloth and instantly fell asleep. Jake and Berry looked at the slumbering ball of fluff and exchanged smiles warm with parental puppy love. He covered her hand with his, and a ripple of excitement rushed through her stomach.

She'd always imagined a good marriage as being comfortable, and a good sexual relationship as being satisfying. Her relationship with Jake Sawyer had a few comfortable moments, but for the most part it was turmoil. And sex was not satisfying. It was exhausting, explosive, ecstatic, overwhelming. Life was hopelessly complicated, she decided. Just when she thought she had something figured out it turned upside down.

She blinked in surprise when a raindrop splashed on her nose. Another hit her forehead. "This has got to be the rainiest April ever," Berry said, helping Jake pack the dishes into the cardboard box. "I still haven't been able to open my apartment windows. The place smells worse than ever."

"I can't say I'm sorry. I like having you in my house."

An awkward feeling squeezed Berry's heart. His words had evoked bittersweet feelings that only intensified the vague apprehension which had settled in her stomach. "Well," she said, feeling clumsy and embarrassed. "Hmm."

Jake rolled the puppy up in the table cloth and handed her to Berry. "You take Calamity Jane."

Berry jumped at the opportunity. Anything for a diversion from the confusing assortment of emotions she was experiencing.

They got to the house just as the rain turned heavy. Jake emptied the box on the kitchen counter and used the carton as a bed for the puppy. She half opened big brown eyes, made a muffled baby-dog sound and went back to sleep.

Jake and Berry tiptoed from the kitchen to the living room, relit the candles, and made a fire in the Franklin stove. Jake plugged a dreamy tape into the stereo system. "Dance?"

Berry moved into the circle of his arms and relaxed against his body, noting how nicely they fit together. Memories of more intimate embraces flooded through her. They knew every square inch of each other. The slope of his hip was imprinted on her palm, the planes of his face embedded in her brain, his hard muscled thigh, the silky triangle of curly black hair, the pulse point at the base of his neck . . . she knew every detail. It was nice to know another human being so thoroughly. It was special. Jake was special, and when she was in his arms like this her world was bliss. She cuddled closer and enjoyed the feel of his hands on her back.

Jake sensuously moved to the music, sometimes softly singing the lyrics in a deep rumbly voice, sometimes whispering outrageous suggestions that made Berry burst into giggles and break into a cold sweat. She wanted Jake Sawyer with a ferocity that shocked her, but she didn't think she could survive a repeat of last Sunday.

The candle flames wavered in pools of molten wax and the logs in the wood stove settled into glowing embers with a soft hiss. The stereo system automatically clicked off, but Jake continued to hold Berry in his arms. They swayed to imaginary tunes, unwilling to break the silken threads that bound them together in perfect harmony.

Berry reluctantly raised her head from his shoulder and cocked an eyebrow as several car doors slammed in the distance, mingling with the muffled sounds of voices.

Jake looked down at Berry with the same puzzled expression. "Were you expecting company?"

The front door lock tumbled and Mrs. Fitz burst into the foyer, followed by Harry Fee, Mildred, Bill Kozinski and a pack of senior citizens.

"You'll never guess!" Mrs. Fitz gestured at Berry and Jake with her apple-dumpling hands. "Mildred and Bill went and got married tonight! Isn't that wonderful?" She hugged Mildred and dabbed at her own red-rimmed eyes. "When they came in to the Pizza Place and told me, I called some friends from the South Side Hotel for Ladies. I thought we should have a party for them. You know, a wedding reception."

Berry's mouth went dry. Mildred and Bill married. How long had they known each other? Two weeks?

Jake's hand was at Berry's elbow, moving her forward. "That's wonderful. Congratulations." He steered Berry towards Mildred and Bill. "Berry and I are very happy for you."

"Berry don't look so happy," Mrs. Fitz said.

"She's surprised," Jake explained.

Berry nodded numbly. "Surprised." She managed a feeble smile. Pull yourself together! she ordered. You're supposed to be happy for them. She had a lump in her throat the size of a basketball, and blind panic raced helter skelter through her brain. Mildred was married. How could she have acted so recklessly? Didn't she know the statistics on divorce? Why would she rush into a relationship that might fail?

Mrs. Fitz looked up a Jake. "Is it all right to have a party? I guess I should have called first, but I got so excited . . ."

Jake grinned. "Of course it's all right to have a party. It's not every day Mildred gets married to my sister's father-in-law." Jake turned to the flustered-looking bridegroom. "Have you called Penny and Frank?"

"Who?"

"Your son. His wife. My sister." Jake rolled his eyes. "Never mind, I'll call them."

An elderly woman with orange hair waved a brown paper sack in the air. "I brought my Chicago tapes. Where's the stereo?"

A case of beer appeared in the foyer. Two stout ladies staggered under a stack of steaming pizza boxes. "Where should we put these?"

Jake winced as the stereo blared rock music. "Good thing I don't have neighbors." He took Berry's hand and led her to the phone. "This hasn't exactly been the evening I'd planned."

"You're being a very good sport about it."

"I'm trying to impress you with my good-humored flexibility. I'm actually screaming inside. I was leading up to a grand finale." He dialed his sister's number and made no attempt to keep the laughter from his voice while he explained the occasion and invited them to the party. He turned back to Berry. "About my grand finale . . ."

Berry suspected she knew about the grand finale. A romantic dinner for two, some very private dancing, and the grand finale: some very passionate sex. She wasn't happy about Mildred getting married, but at least it would postpone the grand finale. She needed time to think. Time away from Jake. "Well, I suppose the grand finale will have to wait awhile. I mean, we can't have a grand finale with all these people around."

Jake looked crestfallen. "I don't suppose we can."

"Gosh, that's too bad," she lied. "I was looking forward to it."

Jake cracked his knuckles. "Me too. I was working myself up to it."

Berry made a face at the play on words. "You sound nervous."

"Scared to death. I've never done it before."

Never done it before? She thought they'd done everything. Everything but . . . "This doesn't involve chains, does it? Or leather stuff?"

Mrs. Fitz bustled past them. "We're out of ice cubes. Isn't this some party?"

"Yeah," Jake scowled, "some party. Wall-to-wall people. Where'd all these people come from? Do we know any of them?"

Berry self-consciously crossed her arms over her

new-found cleavage. "Jake, about this grand finale . . . I'm sort of a traditional person."

"Damn, now I've made you nervous, too." His eyes traveled around the crowded house. "If only we could find some nice quiet place we could still do it."

"Well, ah . . . no sense being hasty about this. Maybe it would be best if we waited."

"Aha!" His face lit up. "The bathroom. We can do it in the bathroom."

"Oh, my god."

Jake draped his arm around her shoulders and pulled her into the powder room adjacent to the kitchen. He locked the door behind him and shoved his hands into his pockets. "Um, maybe you'd better sit down."

Berry looked at the only possible seat and cracked her knuckles. "Do I have to sit? I mean, couldn't we start out standing?"

"Sure. I just thought—this is a little awkward."

Awkward? This wasn't awkward. It was insane. The man had flipped. She must have flipped too. Why else would she have followed him in here?"

Jake looked thoughtful. "I'm not sure how to begin."

Oh, boy, this was going to be another disaster. She could feel it coming. Her mother had lived for fifty-two years without ever losing a mitten, much less a car. Her mother had a sane orderly life that never included exploding cereal, burning apartments or being locked in the bathroom with a crazy man. How did it happen that someone who'd inherited those sensible Scandinavian genes could be fated to stumble through life in such an absurd fashion? "Listen, Jake, it isn't exactly that I have anything against doing it in the bathroom. After all, it was great in the shower, but this is different. This is sort of . . . um, strange."

Jake's brows shot up in astonishment. A roguish grin spread across his face. "You think I brought you in here to ravish your body?"

"Of course not. That's ridiculous." She bit her lip. "Well, yes."

Mischief sparkled in his eyes. "Honey, that's so naughty."

Berry's cheeks flamed. "What the devil did you bring me in here for?"

"To propose."

She closed the lid and sat down with a thud. "Maybe I'll sit down after all."

Jake took a small blue velvet box from his pocket and assumed the traditional proposal position of kneeling on one knee. "Barry, will you . . ."

There was a knock at the door.

"Occupied!" Jake shouted. He popped the ring box open and a huge diamond twinkled at Berry. "I'd like to take more time with this, but someone wants to use the bathroom." He quickly slipped the ring on her limp finger. "Will you marry me?"

Berry sat absolutely mute, staring at the ring in dazed disbelief. What if she actually married him? Someday her children would ask how she got engaged, and she'd have to tell them it was while she was sitting on the toilet. Her mother got engaged at a church picnic. Her sister got engaged in a fancy restaurant. Lingonberry Knudsen got engaged in the bathroom.

Jake patted her hand. "Too excited to speak?"

Berry opened her mouth, but no words emerged. Her mind was a blank. They hadn't invented words yet that suited this occasion.

"You feel okay? You're not going to faint, are you?"

Faint? Faint was the last thing she'd do. She was recovering from the shock, and she was damn mad. She was so mad her skin felt clammy and two bright red spots stained her cheeks. She clenched her fists and pressed her lips together.

Jake took a step backwards. "Uh oh, you're mad."

"You bet I'm mad. You know damn well I don't want to get married. And that was the all-time worst proposal anyone ever made."

"I had a speech prepared, but some senior citizen has to use the facility."

Berry made an attempt to remove the ring but couldn't get it past her knuckle. "It won't come off!" she wailed.

"You've been twisting it, and you've got your finger all swollen."

"In a minute I'm going to make your nose all swollen."

"Don't you want to get married?"

"I have a plan—"

"Me, too."

"I know about your plan. House, spouse, dogs, kids."

"Doesn't your plan include those things?"

"Yes, but—"

He kissed her on the nose. "See? No problem."

"No problem?" she shrieked. "Number one," she ticked off on her finger, "the timing is all wrong. Number two, what about love?"

"Do you love me?"

Berry swallowed. She'd walked right into that one. Did she love him? Of course she loved him, the big dope. She wouldn't be so mad if she didn't love him. If she didn't love him she could smile and graciously reject his offer. If she didn't love him she could appreciate the humor of the situation. But she did love him, and she was mad because he was forcing her hand, making her come to terms with her life-style, making her dissatisfied with her plan. How dare he disrupt her life with all this happiness. Besides, it wasn't her love she was worried about. Suppose she was just a way of achieving the last item on his checklist— kids. "Do you love me?"

"I asked you first."

Berry narrowed her eyes.

Jake wrapped his arms around her and kissed the top of her head. "Of course I love you."

Berry recognized it as his silly-goose tone. It was actually a very loving inflection. Under different circumstances Berry might have found it touching, but at this particular moment she found it inadequate. She would settle for nothing less than passionately romantic. This was no trivial matter. We're talking memories here. We're talking future. She had no intention of having another four-year marriage. The next husband would be chosen more wisely. He would be for keeps.

There was another loud rap at the door.

Jake unlocked the door and ushered Berry past a plump, grey haired lady. "Sorry we took so long," he apologized.

"Merciful heavens," the woman exclaimed in a sharp intake of breath. She looked disapprovingly at Berry and slammed the door.

Berry felt her cheeks redden. "She thought . . ."

Mrs. Fitz suddenly appeared, shaking her finger. "I saw the two of you come out of the bathroom together. What the devil were you doing in there?"

Jake held Berry's hand up to display the ring. "Getting engaged."

"That's wonderful!" Mrs. Fitz said, clasping her plump pink hands to her chest.

Berry snatched her hand away. "Actually, we were only talking about getting engaged. I don't think—"

"Listen up, everyone," Mrs. Fitz shouted. "Berry and Jake got engaged."

A pretty brunette extended her hand to Berry. "I'm Jake's sister, Penny. I'm so relieved to see Jake's finally fallen in love. We thought it'd never happen."

"Really?" Berry could have kicked herself for sounding so pleased. She hadn't meant to sound pleased. She'd meant to inform Penny that they weren't engaged at all, but instead she'd gurgled. Damn.

Penny grinned at her older brother. "Everyone in the family's tried to find a girl for Mr. Picky, here, but nothing doing. Jake always said he'd know when the right one came along, and he wasn't going to settle."

Jake slid his arm around Berry. "It's true. I said that."

Berry looked at him sidewise. "Hmmm." A point for Jake Sawyer. At least he didn't do this on a regular basis. She looked at the beautiful ring and felt her stomach turn. This isn't a typical reaction, she thought. Getting engaged isn't supposed to make you nauseous.

Nine

Berry stood in the doorway and watched the last of Mildred's belongings get loaded into the back of the station wagon. She raised a hand and waved. "Good-bye, Mildred," she whispered.

Jake put an arm around her. "Why so sad? Mildred and Bill will have a good life together."

Berry shrugged. She didn't know why she was sad, but she was dangerously close to crying. Mrs. Dugan was gone. Now Mildred was gone. Her newly adopted family was disbanding, and she felt bereft. "Guess I'm pretty silly, huh?"

"Yup." Jake held her close, resting his cheek against her curls.

"It isn't as if I'll never see them again. When Mildred and Bill come back from their honeymoon they'll be working at the Pizza Place just like always."

"Yup."

"And Mrs. Dugan will be home in another week."

"Yup."

"And I'm engaged."

"You make it sound like a dental appointment."

Berry turned to face him. "I don't want you to take this personally, but I hate being engaged. It upsets my stomach."

Jake's forehead wrinkled into a frown. "You don't want me to take that personally?"

"I didn't sleep a wink last night. I lay there all night long thinking about the dog, the house, the ring . . . you. It's like a dream come true. Everything I've always wanted has suddenly been dropped at my feet."

"So what's the problem?"

"Every time I look at this ring I get nauseous."

"Maybe you have the flu."

"Maybe my stomach is smarter than my brain. Maybe it's trying to tell me something."

Jake's mouth crinkled into a lopsided grin. "Are you serious about this?"

"You think I'm crazy, huh?"

"The word fruitcake did flit through my mind."

Berry nervously twisted the ring on her finger. "But my stomach . . ."

"Don't listen to your stomach. Stomachs are stupid."

Berry's attention turned to the leggy kitten that strolled across the front lawn. "If it hadn't been for that cat . . ."

"Rrrrrf!" Calamity Jane appeared in the doorway and raced down the lawn after the cat. The puppy stopped seven inches from the surprised kitten and bounced around. *"Rrrrf. Rrrrrf."*

The kitten narrowed its eyes and swiped at the dog's nose. Jane yelped and bolted for the house, stopping briefly in the foyer to relieve herself.

"No!" Berry shouted. "Not on the new rug!"

The puppy looked from Berry to Jake and wagged her tail tentatively.

Berry scooped up the floppy-eared ball of fluff. "I think she'd sorry."

Just them Mrs. Fitz thundered down the stairs. "Where's that miserable dog? If I get hold of her there's gonna be dog stew. Look at what she did." Mrs. Fitz waved a mangled piece of brown leather at Berry. "That blasted animal ate my pocketbook." She stopped short and wrinkled her nose. "Phew. What's that smell?"

"The puppy had an accident."

"That does it. I'm not living in no house with puppy smells. Good thing I've got plans."

Berry raised her eyebrows. "Plans?"

Mrs. Fitz beamed. "Harry's on his way over here. He borrowed his son's motor home for a week, and we're gonna go see the Grand Canyon. I've never been there. I was worried about going away and leaving you alone at the Pizza Place, but Jake said it was okay. He said the two of you could handle it just fine."

"Jake knew about this?"

"Mrs. Fitz discussed it with me this morning while you were in the shower. I knew you wouldn't want to stand in the way of the Grand Canyon."

"Well, no, of course not, but what about the lunch contracts? I can't handle the lunch contracts alone, and you'll be teaching."

Jake opened the patio door to let some air into the house. "My teaching career has been cut short. Mrs. Newfarmer is feeling better, and she's returning to her class on Monday."

Berry jammed her fists onto her hips. "Nobody ever tells me anything. Why am I always the last to know what's going on around here?"

Mrs. Fitz pressed her lips together. "Because you either got your nose in a schoolbook or your hand in the refrigerator. And when you're not doing either of those, you're in the shower. Never seen anybody take so many showers. It's a wonder you haven't grown webbed feet."

"Um, showers relax me."

Jake looked at her sidewise.

"Sometimes they relax me."

A horn tooted outside, and Mrs. Fitz scrambled back upstairs. "That's Harry. Tell him I'll be right there. I'm just going to fetch my things."

Berry held tight to Jake's hand. "Mrs. Fitz is leaving! Do something."

"I offered to help with her luggage, but she said she was traveling light."

Berry grunted in exasperation. "I'm not talking about luggage. I'm talking about Mrs. Fitz and Harry. We have to stop them."

"Why?"

"Because . . ." Berry bit her lip. "Why? There are lots of good reasons."

"Uh-huh."

"They're old. What if they have a heart attack going through the dessert? What if Mrs. Fitz forgets her blood pressure medicine? What if she can't find prune juice?"

"You sound like June Cleaver waiting for Wally to come home from his first date."

"Hell." She sat on the lowest step, resting her elbows on her knees, and her chin in her hands. Okay, Berry, she thought, what's the real because? Because I don't want to live all alone in this terrific house with Jake. Things were happening too fast. One minute she was delivering pizza to Quasimodo and three weeks later she was engaged. Her stomach told her to take the ring off, but she couldn't—it was stuck. Stuck on her swollen finger, stuck to her love-struck heart. What a mess.

Mrs. Fitz sidled past her wearing jeans and a backpack. "What do you think?" she said modeling her outfit. "Harry got these duds for me. Pretty nice, huh?" Harry waved from the front door, and Mrs. Fitz hugged Berry. "Boy, this is gonna be great. Harry and I are gonna live in sin and see the Grand Canyon all at the same time. Ain't that something?"

Berry followed Mrs. Fitz to the front porch and watched the motor home rumble away. "When I grow up I want to be just like Mrs. Fitz."

Jake tipped his head back and let out a great peal of laughter. "Me too!" he said, wiping his eyes. "I especially like the living in sin part."

The sound of glass breaking reached their ears, and they turned and looked at each other quizzically. Another crash, followed by puppy footsteps scuttling up the basement stairs. Both cat and dog burst through the cellar door and ran straight for Berry and Jake.

Jake snared Jane and carried her into the house. "Didn't I lock this dog in the kitchen?"

Berry stared in amazement at the pile of splintered wood that used to be the "puppy proof" gate blocking the kitchen doorway. "She ate her way out. Ugh, what's that smell?"

Jake's voice faltered. "I don't notice any smell."

"Are you kidding me? Any minute now the paint's going to start peeling off the walls. It smells like . . . it smells like my apartment!"

"That's impossible."

"I'd know that stench anywhere. It reminds me of rotten fish in a gym locker." Her face reflected total bafflement, and then the significance of the familiar odor began to register in her mind. She held a kitchen towel across her nose and headed for the basement. "That smell is coming from your lab."

Jake took the towel from her with grim determination. "I'll go down and survey the damage." Seconds later he rushed up the stairs and slammed the door behind him, gasping for air and grinning sheepishly. The expression on his flushed face was half embarrassed little boy and half unrepentant pirate. "Looks like the animals chased each other around some down there and knocked over a few beakers. Nothing dangerous, but this house is going to smell like a dead groundhog for a few days. Even if I shut all the vents and doors, the fumes will still travel through the air-conditioning system."

Berry clenched her teeth and stalked out of the house. She'd been embarrassingly slow to catch on, but she finally had all the pieces in place. That stinking odor had kept her from returning to her apartment . . . and it was manufactured in Jake Sawyer's cellar. "If there's one thing I can't stand," she shouted at him, "it's a sneaky chemist!"

"Boy, you're cute when you're mad."

"Ugh." She thunked her forehead with her fist and shoved Jane at him. "Take your dog. I'm leaving. I'm going home to my rancid apartment."

This is why you don't marry a man you've only known for two weeks, she thought with a snarl. He could turn out to be a slimeball. He could be conniving and unscrupulous and manipulative. He could make a complete ass out of you. She threw her hands into the air and ranted as she charged down Ellenburg Drive. "How could I have been so stupid? So gullible? I was putty in his hands. Him and his damn soapy fingers and stupefying kisses." She should have listened to her stomach. You could always count on your stomach to know these things.

A car horn beeped behind her. It was him. "Go away!"

"Want a ride?"

"NO!" She refused to turn her head, but she could hear the car creeping along behind her. Finally she lost patience. "Why are you following me?"

He waved her purse out the window. "You forgot your key."

Berry flushed and reached for the purse, but he withdrew it and patted the seat beside him. "Why are you so mad?"

"You tricked me."

"Only a little. In the beginning your apartment smelled bad all by itself."

"You've probably lied to me about all sorts of things. You've probably got a wife somewhere. Kids. More dogs."

"Rrrrf." Calamity Jane sat like the king of the mountain on a pile of clothes thrown across the back seat.

Berry looked at the clothes and the dog with increasing uneasiness. "What's all this stuff?"

"Our clothes."

"What are our clothes doing in your car?"

Jake smiled pleasantly. "I'm taking them to your apartment. I thought since my house is unlivable, we'd stay at your place for awhile."

"We? Like in you, me and the dog? Are you crazy?"

"Probably. Get in."

Berry wrenched the door open and sat down with a defiant thud. She grabbed her purse and clutched it to her chest, her mouth a tight line of fury, her eyes staring straight ahead in unblinking indignation. "You are not staying in my apartment."

"Why not?"

"Because. It wouldn't look right."

Jake made a derisive snorting sound.

Berry narrowed her eyes. "And I'm certainly not harboring a man who makes snorting sounds when I'm trying to answer a question."

"Harbor? I like that. Is that like, he slipped his tugboat into the snug harbor?"

Berry bobbed her head back and forth. "Just what I'd expect from a sex fiend."

"Sex fiend? Me?" He pursed his lips for a moment and then smiled. "Gee, thanks."

"That wasn't a compliment," she ground out. "I suppose it's difficult to figure those things out when you think with your dingdong."

"Listen, Peeping Berry, I think this is the pot calling the kettle black. After all, I wasn't the one who fell out of a tree trying to get a gander at a thinking dingdong."

He didn't even have the grace to take this seriously, she raged. He kept smiling, sitting there making glib remarks in mock indignation. It made her even more infuriated. If she had her way his ding would never dong again.

Jake parked in front of the Pizza Place and reached behind him for Calamity Jane. He grabbed an armful of clothes and waited patiently while the puppy wandered aimlessly around on the sidewalk. "Maybe she's empty," he said after a few minutes of no action.

"That dog is never empty, and she's not living in my apartment. And neither are you."

"Hear that, Jane? She's going to turn us out in the cold. When she was homeless I let her live in my house. I even let her bring her three old ladies . . . and I never once asked If they were housebroken."

"Why can't you live with your sister?"

"She's allergic to dogs. They give her hives and make her wheeze."

Berry closed her eyes and sighed loudly. "I'll give you three days, maximum. The rules are that you sleep in the living room and you don't talk to me."

Jake waggled his eyebrows. "We've got it made," he whispered to the dog. "She didn't say anything about my sex fiend activities."

Berry opened windows that were still barren of curtains. How depressing. After the fire damage had been repaired she'd furnished her apartment with only the bare necessities. She and the ladies had lovingly hung curtains in Jake's house. They'd shopped for rugs and kitchen chairs and houseplants for the old Victorian house, but they hadn't found the time to buy a new couch for the apartment. Shame on me, Berry thought, I've deserted my home for greener pastures . . . for a roll in the hay and butterscotch pudding.

And it was worth it, she realized with a start. Living in Jake's house had been a long overdue treat. She'd worked hard, and she'd needed a vacation, but now it was over. Time to come back to the real world.

She stood still as a statue for a moment absorbing her thoughts. Was that what it was? A couple of weeks in the country? A romantic fling? Jake Sawyer's bed-and-breakfast. She twisted the beautiful ring on her finger and swallowed back a lump in her throat. For a very short time it had seemed like much more than a fling. Oh brother, now she was getting sad. She really had to get a grip on her emotions. And she had to get rid of the ring. Most likely she was so emotional because she was engaged. Engagements and puppies were hell on hormones.

Berry stood at the sink and slathered her finger with soap, but the ring wouldn't budge. She heard Jake trudging up the stairs with another armful of clothes and felt her stomach churn. He was actually moving in with her in this teeny efficiency. No ladies for chaperons. No lock on the bathroom door. No place to hide. She would have to rely on her self-control and his sense of honor. Swell.

And if that wasn't bad enough, she wasn't even

mad anymore. Anger had been replaced with panic. Pure, unadulterated heart-thumping panic . . . which, surprisingly enough, felt a lot like lust. Berry commanded herself to think of something else. The ring. Butter. She frantically hunted in the refrigerator for butter. Eggs, yogurt, cantaloupe. No butter. She searched the cabinets and found a bottle of cooking oil. "Aha!"

Jake looked on with interest. "Oil?"

"Don't get your hopes up."

"You're oiling your finger?"

"My ring finger." She placed her thumb and forefinger under the slippery ring and gave a good push, and the gold band flew off her finger like the cork from a champagne bottle.

Jake watched the diamond sail through the air and sink into the new carpet. "Too small?"

"Too sudden. I'm not ready to be engaged."

His voice was as soft as his touch as he reached out for her, tugging at a curl, sliding fingertips across the nape of her neck. "Yes, you are. You're ready for all kinds if things . . . to give love, to get loved, to have puppies."

Berry's eyes opened wide. "Good grief." She clapped one hand over her mouth and pointed to Jane. "She just ate the ring."

Jake looked skeptically at the little dog. "That's impossible."

"Honest to goodness, I think she swallowed the ring."

Jake dropped to his knees and raked his hand through the carpet. "Jane, you canine garbage pail, tell me you didn't eat that expensive, undigestible ring."

"Oh lord, what's going to happen to her?" Berry carefully cradled the fat puppy. "Will she be all right? Will she die? Dogs can't eat rings, can they?"

"To begin with, we're not even sure if she ate the ring."

They crawled around on the rug for several minutes, searching in vain for the diamond.

Berry had difficulty finding her voice. "It's not here. Maybe we should take her to a vet."

Jake stroked a soft, floppy ear. "I suppose we should."

Berry held the dog close and headed for the stairs. "There's a veterinary clinic just a block from here. I pass it on my way to school. I think it's one of those twenty-four-hour emergency things so maybe it will be open on Sunday." Please be open on Sunday, she prayed. This was all her fault. If she hadn't had the damn ring all slickered up with oil it wouldn't have smelled like food. The puppy whimpered and wriggled in Berry's arms. "It's okay, Jane. We're almost there. The vet will know what to do."

Jake opened the clinic door to an empty well-lit waiting room. "Guess there's not much happening in the veterinary world on Sunday morning."

The receptionist glanced up from her typing and smiled. "We don't schedule appointments on Sunday. Only emergency cases. Is this an emergency?"

"We think the puppy ate a ring. A big expensive ring."

The receptionist nodded sympathetically. "That could be an emergency." She gave Jake a card to fill out. "I'll get Dr. Pruett."

"I hope Dr. Pruett knows what he's doing," Berry whispered to Jake. "Maybe we should have taken Jane to a specialist."

"Maybe we should have taken her to a jeweler." Jake slid an arm around Berry's shoulders. "Honey, she's going to be fine."

"I know."

"Then why is that tear hanging onto your eyelashes?"

"Poor Jane. She's just a baby, and she has a scratchy ring inside her."

Jake cradled Berry in his arms, being careful not to squash the panting puppy. "You love her, huh?"

Berry sobbed a strangled "Yes," and buried her face in his shoulder. "Why does love always have to be so painful?"

"It's not always painful." He tenderly kissed her temple. "Jane probably thinks love is pretty great. She's so happy to be getting all this attention and affection, she probably doesn't even notice that silly ring in her stomach."

Berry let her cheek rest against his chest. "You think so?" It was a nice thought, that she could make Jane feel better just by loving her.

The receptionist beckoned from the hallway. "Mr. and Mrs. Sawyer, you can take Jane into Examining Room Two. Dr. Pruett will be right with you."

Berry started to correct her, but changed her mind. Mrs. Sawyer. Berry Sawyer. It had a certain sound to it. She caught Jake smiling at her and made an impatient noise with her teeth. Lord, the man was impossible. He didn't miss a thing, damn him.

Dr. Pruett was a short, stocky man with a receding hairline and an obvious love of puppies. He scratched Jane's neck while he took her temperature and told her dog jokes when he examined her teeth. "She seems to be in perfect health," he told Jake and Berry, "With the exception of possibly having a diamond stuck somewhere in her gizzards." He tucked Jane under his arm. "I'm going to take a couple of X rays. We'll be right back."

"X rays," Berry worried, "that sounds so serious. And do you suppose they're safe? She'd just a baby."

Jake rolled his eyes. "Open your mouth and let me examine your teeth and I'll tell you jokes about Scandinavians."

Ten minutes later Dr. Pruett returned with Jane and proudly displayed her X rays. "There it is! She swallowed the ring, all right. It's lodged in her stomach." He turned to Jake. "Looks to me like you're engaged to a cocker spaniel."

Berry gripped Jake's hand. "Does she have to be operated on?"

Dr. Pruett stroked the glossy black ears. "There's a good chance that she'll pass the ring all by herself. If you like, you can leave Jane here for a day or two. We'll keep a real close watch on her and feed her a little mineral oil to help ease things along."

Berry nodded numbly. "You'll call us if anything . . . happens?"

WUMP. Berry slammed the wad of pizza dough onto the butcher-block table and punched it with her fist.

Jake watched out of the corner of his eye and flinched. "You're not very big, but you sure do pack a wallop."

THWUP. Berry hit it with the rolling pin. "I get rid of my frustrations this way."

"You must be really frustrated. You've been beating up on that dough all day." He leaned across the table at her. "You want to know how I get rid of my frustrations?"

"No!"

"Are these frustrations of yours physical in nature?"

"No."

His voice gentled. "Want to talk about it?"

Berry sighed and pushed her curls behind her ears, leaving white flour smudges on her flushed cheeks. "No." What was there to talk about? She was confused and scared. Cold feet, that's what she had.

Jake slouched against the counter. "I hate to ruin your fun, but it's ten o'clock. We've had three customers in the past two hours, and you've got enough pizza crusts to last through November. What do you say we call it a night?"

Berry looked up from her pounding. "It's ten o'clock already?"

His silky voice held a teasing challenge. "If I didn't know better, I'd guess you were avoiding going to bed with me."

Berry dusted her hands off on her apron and tipped her nose defiantly into the air. "That's absurd. And I'm not going to bed with you. We're going to bed separately. I go into my bedroom, shut my door, and go to sleep. You sleep . . . somewhere else."

"Where else am I supposed to sleep? You don't even have a couch."

"That's your problem." Lord, she felt like a rat. He'd been so sweet to her all day, all week—ever since they'd met. Why did she feel compelled to push him away? She must be nuts. No woman in her right mind would pass up Jake Sawyer.

She hung the CLOSED sign in the door and locked up, mentally reviewing her linens. She had an extra sheet and blanket. Everything else was at his place. A sheet and blanket would have to do.

They reached the top of the stairs and sniffed.

"Smells nice," Jake offered. "Smells like fresh pizza crust."

"No thanks to you."

There was a subtle play of emotions across his

face. His mouth tightened and a muscle twitched in his jaw. "Do you have an extra blanket?"

Berry went to the freshly painted linen closet and gave him the extra sheet and almost thread-bare blue blanket. "I'm sorry I don't have a better blanket." She heard her voice falter and quickly turned before he could see the tears that were gathering behind her eyes. She stiffened her back and briskly strode to her bedroom, closing the door behind her.

Berry leaned against the door and for the first time realized why the term "heartache" had been coined. The emotional anguish she was experiencing was so intense it had become a physical pain that squeezed her heart and forced air into her lungs in shallow gasps. She flung herself onto the bed and muffled her sobs in the pillow.

Why was love so complicated for her? She'd always thought of herself as a fairly well-adjusted, heart-on-her-sleeve, giving type of person. She fed stray dogs, took in stranded old ladies, and rescued kittens.

Now, suddenly she was all closed up and afraid to love. And the very worst part was that she was being mean to Jake. For a split second, when she'd handed him the blanket, she'd caught a glimpse of the pain and confusion her rejection had caused. It had reminded her of poor Calamity Jane, sitting all alone in a veterinarian's wire cage. The little dog must be wondering what she had done to deserve such punishment.

The lights clicked off in the other room, and Berry lay absolutely still on her bed, trying to sort through the muddle of conflicting feelings. What we have here are two entirely different kinds of people, she thought. Jake is a risk-taker—a man who trusts his instincts.

She sat up and stared at her shoes. Running

shoes. A trustworthy brand. Not too cheap, not too expensive. Middle-of-the-road shoes, she decided. I've worn middle-of-the-road shoes all my life, and I've never been really sure where they were taking me until a year ago when I went back to school and bought the Pizza Place.

She could still remember how difficult it had been to borrow the money. She had no collateral and no business experience, but she had confidence in herself. Berry removed her socks and ruefully thought that she'd gone through a lot of banks before she found one that was willing to invest in her confidence. Now, thanks to the lunch contracts, her pizza business was in the black. She'd made a sound business decision and stuck by it and succeeded.

Maybe her upset stomach had something to do with success. Success felt good. Failure felt bad. Marriage had been a dismal failure, and she was so scared of failing at another marriage that she was afraid to take a chance. Berry wrinkled her nose. She didn't like the way that sounded. What's happened to my confidence? she fumed. Is this any way for a successful pizza tycoon to act?

Berry quietly opened her bedroom door and peered out at Jake. He was asleep on the floor, on his back, one arm flung over his head. Moonlight spilled through the open window, illuminating his face, highlighting the curves of his body under the thin blanket. She shook her head. Is this any way to treat the man you love? She removed the quilt from her bed and tucked it in around Jake.

Tomorrow morning she would get up bright and early and make him pancakes. And she would talk to him. She couldn't talk to him before because she hadn't figured it out. Now she had it all straight in her mind. Fear of failure. Her plan had put marriage at the end of the line so she wouldn't goof up any sooner than necessary. What kind of a plan is that? she asked herself. A coward's plan.

She stuck her chin out and marched back to her bedroom. Lingonberry Knudsen was no coward. Tomorrow she was going to have a long talk with herself and straighten this mess out. Then she was going to talk to Jake.

Ten

Berry opened one eye and sniffed. Someone was cooking bacon. She snatched at the digital clock on her nightstand and squinted at it. Someone was cooking bacon at five o'clock in the morning. She ran her hand through her unruly curls, wrapped a short terry robe over her University of Washington nightshirt and shuffled out to the kitchen.

Jake waved a spatula at her in greeting.

"What on earth are you doing?"

"Making us breakfast. I knew the smell of bacon would get you stumbling out here."

"It's five in the morning. Couldn't you get me stumbling out at seven or eight?"

"Have you forgotten what day this is? This is not an ordinary day."

"Um, of course I know what day this is." My birthday? His birthday? The beginning of National Pickle Week? What is he talking about?

Jake poured Berry a cup of coffee and set a plate of scrambled eggs, a buttered muffin, and half a pound of bacon in front of her. "Isn't this the day you take your art history exam?"

"Good lord. My exam."

"I know you've been studying for it all week, and then you had sort of a disruptive weekend. So I thought you'd probably want to get up early and do some last-minute cramming." He plunked her school notebook beside her plate.

He got her up early to study art history! Berry felt her eyes getting misty. When the right man came along, he didn't stop you from achieving your goals. He encouraged you to be successful. That's why their marriage was going to work, she thought dreamily, because Jake was going to help her make it a success.

Jake cocked an eyebrow at her. "You have the strangest expression on your face. Are you feeling okay?"

"I'm feeling wonderful. I'm going to eat this entire scrumptious breakfast, then I'm going to study my brains out until two o'clock, and when I come back from my exam . . ."

Jake sat opposite her and began nibbling on his own half a pound of bacon. "When you come back from your exam, if I'm not mistaken, you're going to have to study economics."

He was right. She had her economics exam tomorrow morning. Good thing she only had two courses this semester. She didn't think she could put off attacking him much longer than Wednesday.

At ten o'clock the phone rang. "It's Dr. Pruett," Jake called to Berry. "Good news. The ring is in Jane's intestines. Not long now!"

Berry tipped her head back and laughed softly as happiness flowed through her. Everything in her life was turning out right. She'd probably ace her art history exam. She didn't know why she was bothering to study. "You sound like an expectant father, waiting for your spaniel to deliver a healthy two-karat ring."

Jake shook his head in amazement. "Two months ago if anyone had told me I'd be this worried over a dog, I'd have told them they were crazy."

"She'll be fine."

His eyes watched her intently. "Something strange is going on here. That was my line last night. Now you're reassuring me."

"That's because I feel fine." She shook her pencil at him for emphasis. "Not everyone can be a successful pizza tycoon."

"That's what's important to you, huh? Being a pizza tycoon?"

Berry buried her nose in her art book. "Nope. I don't give a fig about pizza. It's the success part."

Jake stared at her for a moment, lost in thought. He nodded slightly, as if he understood, and kissed her lightly on the top of her head. "I don't give a fig about pizza either. Nevertheless, I shall now descend to the bowels of the Pizza Place and work my little fingers to the bone fulfilling lunch contracts. Do you know why I'm going to do this?"

Berry giggled at his self-sacrificing voice. "No. Why are you going to do this?"

His eyes were filled with mischief. "Because I have to pay the price. I got rid of your ladies for the express purpose of getting you into the sack, and now that I've boinked the pizza tycoon I have to pay the piper."

Berry's art history book sailed through the air and hit the opposite wall with an resounding thud, but Jake Sawyer had already ducked around the corner and was halfway down the stairs.

Berry gave the door to the Pizza Place a shove and staggered to the counter where Jake was working. "One more slide of sixteenth-century bucolic splendor, and my eyes will fall out of my head."

Jake wiped his hands on his apron and grinned. "Tough exam?"

"I don't know. My mind is numb." She held her hand up. "I can't let go of my pencil."

"Poor Berry," he gasped, trying to smother his laughter as he pried the pencil from her fingers. "Good thing you only have one more exam."

"Yeah, good thing." Her attention was diverted by a yelp from the corner of the small restaurant area. "Jane!"

The little black dog was confined in a playpen. She hopped up and down at the sight of Berry. She wagged her tail and made excited puppy sounds and rolled on the plastic playpen mat.

Berry rushed over and hugged Jane. "She remembers me. She's so smart," she bragged to Jake.

"Not only is she smart, but she's also empty, if you know what I mean."

"What a good dog." Berry laid her cheek against the silky black head. "It was so clever of you to . . . um, get rid of that ring."

Jake delivered a salad and a hamburger to the table nearest the playpen. "Come here, Goldilocks. I made you some supper, and then you're excused to go upstairs and study."

"Yum, I'm famished." She plopped the puppy back in the playpen.

"No more upset stomachs?"

"Nope. All gone. I'm fine. Never been better in my whole life."

Jake stiffened. "Great. I suppose that makes you real happy."

"Yup." She munched on a carrot stick and watched Jane attack a rawhide dog chewy. "This playpen is a great idea."

"I borrowed it from my sister. She's one of those family-type people."

Now what? Berry wondered. All of a sudden he sounds absolutely cranky. She ate the last bite of hamburger and stabbed a lone chunk of raw broccoli from her salad bowl. "Well, that was terrific. Guess I'll go hit the books now."

Jake bent over a wad of pizza dough. WUMP. He smacked it with the rolling pin.

Wow, Berry thought, I've never seen him whack pizza dough around like that. Maybe he's cracking under the strain of fatherhood. Maybe he isn't ready to have puppies. Boy, wouldn't that be the pits? Here I am all set to go off and start researching baby food, and Jake gets cold feet. Well, if that's the problem, we'll work it out together. We're a team. She smiled at a scowling Jake and hummed as she went through the door.

Several hours later Berry was startled out of her studying by stomping and thumping on the stairs. Jake swung the collapsed playpen around the corner and unceremoniously tumbled a squirming puppy onto the rug. "Damn, I didn't think I was going to make it. This dog didn't want to hold still."

Berry closed her economics book and stood at her seat by the table. He was still cranky. Can't blame him, she decided. He's had a long day. Up at five to help me study. Worked making pizza for twelve hours. And somewhere in between he's had to be responsible for Jane.

"Rrrrf," Jane squeaked, running in circles, chasing her tail.

Well, all that was about to end. He could relax now. She'd take care of Jane. She'd show him they could be a team and raise puppies by the hundreds. She grabbed Jane and kissed the top of her head. "Has the puppy eaten?"

"She had a pepperoni pizza at about seven."

"Is she allowed to eat that? I mean isn't she on a special diet after her ordeal?"

Jake gave her a black look. "I let her run around loose as a special treat, and she ate some guy's pizza when he went to the john."

"Oh, dear."

"She even ate his napkin."

"Anything else I should know about? How's her stomach?"

"Her stomach's fine. How's your stomach?"

Obviously, he didn't want to talk about the dog. "My stomach's okay."

"Humph." He slouched onto a kitchen chair and turned his attention to the newspaper.

Humph? What kind of an answer was "humph"? How was she supposed to make conversation with a man that said "humph" and then pressed his nose into the sports page? She had to tell him about success and failure and commitment. She was ready for all that stuff. More than ready— practically panting. Marriage would be wonderful this time. She looked at Jake and thought her heart would burst. Lord, she loved him. Allen had been a roommate. Jake was her friend, her lover, her helpmate, her hero. She hugged herself and twirled around, dancing a little jig as she went to the kitchen to fill a water bowl for the puppy.

Jake squinted at her antics over the top of his paper. "Humph," he mumbled, rattling the funnies.

Berry glared down at him. "What's all this 'humph'?"

"It's nothing," he snapped. "I'm just happy to see you so happy."

"Oh." Maybe this wasn't such a good time to talk to him. Poor guy must be exhausted. Berry allowed herself a wicked grin. She knew how to wake him up. She had a slinky little nightie in her drawer that would make him wake up and take notice. She stretched and yawned. "Well, I'm pooped. Guess it's bedtime."

Silence.

"Aren't you tired? Aren't you ready for bed?" she asked hopefully.

"I'd like to read my paper first."

Just as well. She smiled. It would give her time to get ready. This was going to be a night to remember. First, a shower. She did a little strip-tease for herself in the bathroom. *"Ta da,"* she whispered, flinging her shirt behind her. *"Boom da da boom."* She dropped her jeans. "And now, for the grand finale, *'Hubba hubba, rhmmmm.'*" She did an exotic bump-and-grind out of her panties. The steamy water cascaded over her shoulders, running in rivulets down her belly and her long legs. She reverently held a brand-new bar of soap in her hand. And to think, all these years she had been taking showers to get clean.

She lathered herself lavishly, imagining Jake's hands smoothing the slick foam over her shoulders and arms, across her soft breasts. She relathered and generously applied the creamy soap to her light brown curls, experiencing a rush of delight as she touched sensitive private places and anticipated Jake's seeking mouth and insistent fingers. She stood for a long time under the shower spray, enjoying her new-found boldness, relishing the sensations of a woman about to be loved.

When she felt thoroughly ready she stepped from the shower and shook her curls dry. She placed a dab of perfume between her breasts, and on a reckless impulse, added a touch to a strategic spot between her legs. She blushed at the unprecedented action. *Lord, Berry, that's so . . . naughty!* She slipped the filmy black nightie over her head and looked at herself in the mirror. She was decadent. Perfectly decadent. The scoop neck dipped low over the small swell of her breasts, and the hem just skimmed along her bottom barely covering her.

"Well, here goes." She giggled nervously, opening the bedroom door to a darkened living room.

When her eyes adjusted to the dim light she blinked in horror at the inert form stretched out on the floor. Jake was asleep! Berry stood openmouthed, listening to his gentle regular breathing, watching the slow rise and fall of his chest. The puppy slept beside him, curled into a ball, tucked securely under his left armpit. Oh, damn! "Tell me this isn't happening," she muttered. "This is a joke, right?" Wrong. He was asleep. Here she was with perfume on her crowning glory, and Jake Sawyer was asleep. Now what? She could wake him. She could stomp around and bang a few pots and pans, but that didn't seem like a nice thing to do. He looked so peaceful. Well, so much for decadence.

She went back to her bedroom and threw the wicked scrap of nylon into the drawer and tugged a well-worn Seattle Seahawks jersey over her head. "Men!" she snarled, punching her pillow into a shapeless lump. If she lived to be a hundred she'd never know what to expect from a man. Just when you finally decided you wanted them, what did they do? They fell asleep. Well, there would be no more sexy surprises for Jake Sawyer. No sirree. Next time she wanted to make love to him she'd make an appointment and get it in writing. And first thing in the morning she was going to burn that damn nightgown.

She pulled the quilt up to her neck and shut off the lamp on her nightstand. She watched the minutes change on her digital clock. She watched the lights of passing cars reflect on her window shade. She picked the nail polish off her index finger. "I can't sleep," she groaned. "I'm in lust." *Okay, we'll do this scientifically. Relax toes. Relax ankles. Relax knees. Relax thighs. Relax . . . This isn't working.*

She turned onto her stomach and smushed her face into the mattress. She needed something to get her mind off her body. She could worry about Mrs. Dugan. Mrs. Dugan and Harry were wheeling their way south. Berry opened one eye and checked out the clock. What was Mrs. Dugan doing right now? Berry rolled her eyes. They were probably in bed. Together! Damn. She flung herself onto her back and thrashed around until she was hopelessly tangled in the sheet. This was all Jake's fault, the slimeball. How dare he sleep when she was in such a state.

She heard rustling in the living room and a band of light flashed on under her door.

"What the devil?" Jake roared. "Oh, damn!"

Berry thought about it for a minute and reached the obvious conclusion. "Pepperoni pizza?" she called to Jake.

"This is so disgusting. Why does this dog always get sick when I'm around."

Berry hugged herself and curled her toes. What a shame. Now Jake was going to have to take a shower and find another place to sleep. She smoothed the sheets and plumped her pillow.

Jake stormed into the bathroom, muttering colorful phrases, and slammed the door. Minutes later he emerged with damp hair and a towel precariously draped on his hips. He stood at the edge of the bed and peered at Berry in the semi-darkness. "I need another blanket."

Berry wriggled beneath the quilt. "Gee, I don't have any more blankets. They're all at your house."

"Dammit, I can't sleep out there. It's cold, and the floor is hard, and it smells."

He sounds like a truculent four-year-old, Berry thought. How adorable.

"Well?" he asked.

"Well, what?" Said the spider to the fly.

"Well, aren't you going to tell me I can sleep with you. Hell, it's the least you can do. It was your dog that got sick."

"Speaking of my dog, where is the little darling?"

"I put her in the playpen."

"Hmmm."

"That's it? Hmmm?"

Berry scooted over to the other side of the bed. "Okay. I suppose you're right about the dog. I mean, there isn't really any other place to sleep." *Goody goody goody.* She placed her hand on her chest when she heard his towel drop to the floor. Holy cow. Be still my heart.

Jake slid under the quilt and turned to Berry. "Listen, Berry—" He sighed heavily and rolled away from her. "Oh, hell."

Something was going wrong here, Berry thought. She was in bed with a naked man, and he just turned his back on her. She understood about being tired, but this was going too far. This was getting insulting. So, the hell with him. Damned if she'd go salivating after his precious body when he didn't give a fig about hers. "Humph," she snorted, rolling away from him. She straightened her nightshirt. She straightened the sheet. She shaped her pillow just so.

"Berry."

"You growled?"

"What are you doing? Practicing the polka?"

"I can't get comfortable. I'm not used to sharing my bed."

"No joke."

Berry sat bolt upright. "What's that supposed to mean?"

"It means I'm very well aware of the fact that you prefer to sleep alone."

"You make abstinence sound like a social disease."

"I think abstinence is dandy. I think you've elevated mental virginity to a new high."

"Ugh." Berry smacked him with her pillow.

Jake snatched the pillow from her and tucked it under his head.

"Jake Sawyer, give me back my pillow!"

"Possession is nine tenths of the law. It's mine now."

Berry ripped the quilt from him and wrapped herself in it cocoon style, gloating over the gasp of surprise she'd provoked. Two could play this game. He wasn't the only one who was capable of acting childish.

Jake grabbed an end and dumped her out of the quilt.

"Hey, possession is nine tenths of the law!"

"Only when you're big and strong like me." He placed the pillow in the middle of the bed and pointed with his finger. "That half of the pillow is yours." He draped the quilt over them and tucked her in. "How's your stomach?"

"It's fine. How's yours?" What was with this stomach stuff? That had to be the third time tonight he'd asked about her stomach.

"Mmmph." He slammed his head onto his half of the pillow.

Berry jumped out of his way and propped herself up on one elbow. "Um, Jake?"

"Yeah."

"We don't fit like this. I can't get my head onto my half of the pillow. Your shoulders are too yum . . . er, too big."

He silently rolled to his side, and Berry inched

her way over. Now they were back to back, tush to tush. Berry watched the digital minutes tick by. She couldn't sleep like this. Tush to tush was uncomfortable. She held her breath and very carefully rolled over until she was facing Jake, spoon-fashion. Yes, she decided, this was much better.

For lack of something better to do with her arm, she draped it over his waist and rested her cheek just millimeters from his neck. Mmmm, she was getting more comfortable all the time, but the angle was wrong. She was sure she could go to sleep if she were just a bit closer, so she wriggled around until she was perfectly molded to Jake's back. She finally had attained the ideal position for sleep, and she was so pleased about it that she allowed herself a sigh of satisfaction. "Ahhh," she sighed softly, blowing a little wisp of warm air across his neck, into his ear.

"Ohhh . . ."

"Pardon?" she whispered, her voice husky with thoughts of sleep.

Jake's voice cracked when he spoke. "Are you comfortable?"

Berry stretched slightly, pressing her breasts into his back. "Mmmm. Are you?"

There was a low groan and she felt the muscles in his buttocks tense. She shifted position, causing the hem of the nightshirt to creep up, exposing a bare thatch of silky brown curls. "I'm so tired, I can hardly keep my eyes open. How about you?" she asked, sliding the curls across the dark crevice of Jake's second best feature.

"I'm not tired at all. To tell you the truth, I'm wide awake. In fact, I'm getting more awake by the minute."

Berry's finger carelessly stroked the center of Jake's belly. "Maybe, you just need some relaxing."

"Relax? With your nipples poking into my back

and your finger stuck in my navel?" He gave a sigh of desperation and turned around to face her. "Listen, Berry, there's something I have to tell you."

Berry felt his arousal hard and full against her, cleverly sneaking its way under her nightshirt. She ran her hands across his smooth muscular back and kissed the pulse point that throbbed in his neck. She loved him. With all her heart and soul and every hormone she possessed. She loved the way he got excited about his crazy food inventions, and the way he accepted the ladies. He could bandage a scratch, inflate a sagging ego, make a helluva pepperoni pizza, and turn her into mush with a single glance. "I have a few things to tell you, too. The first thing I need to tell you is that I'm going to make mad, passionate love to you."

Jake's thumb teased a taut, dusky nipple. "And the second thing?"

Berry caught her lower lip between her teeth and concentrated on the sweet agony his thumb was causing. "The second thing?"

Eleven

Berry was sure if she got any happier she would begin to purr. It was a wonderful luxury to awaken in the arms of your lover, she thought. Especially when your lover was about to become your husband and the father of your children. At least she assumed he was about to become her husband and the father of the children. Actually, he hadn't mentioned marriage last night. And now that she thought about it, he hadn't returned the ring. She pressed her cheek to his chest and listened to the steady beat of his heart while he slept. Good thing she was secure and not the sort to panic. If she was the sort to panic she might worry that he's caught cold feet from her.

There was a squeal of brakes on the street and the angry slam of a car door. "And another thing," a familiar voice shouted. "I don't snore. You snore!"

Mrs. Fitz? Berry rolled out of bed and went to the window.

"What the devil are you doing here? Why aren't you at the house?" Mrs. Fitz shouted up to her.

"It's a long story. Why aren't you on your way to the Grand Canyon?"

Mrs. Fitz flapped her arms at the departing camper. "You ever try to live in one of them things with an old man? It was enough to take seven years off my life. He drives like a maniac. He makes disgusting slurping noises at breakfast. And I can't stand the way he blows his nose. He honks. You don't have to honk when you blow your nose." She fished in her purse and inserted her key in the door. "Boy, it's good to be home. I can't wait to make myself a cup of tea."

"I just had the scariest dream," Jake said, sitting up in bed. "I thought I heard Mrs. Fitz saying it was good to be home."

Berry slumped against the wall. "That was no dream. Harry slurped and honked, so Mrs. Fitz dumped him." She pulled on a pair of jeans and dropped a yellow T-shirt over her head. "I'll make coffee and you can take Jane for a walk."

"Old men," Mrs. Fitz muttered in the kitchen. "Don't ever go camping with an old man. Nothing but a pain in the behind."

"I thought you and Harry got along so well."

"Yeah, well, you never really know a man until you've had to sit across from him at the breakfast table."

Berry leaned against the counter while the coffee dripped. "Jake is sensational at the breakfast table."

"Yeah. After you've eaten breakfast with Jake, you're ruined."

Voices carried up to them from the street. Berry and Mrs. Fitz looked at each other and raised their eyebrows when the downstairs door opened.

"Better not be Harry coming back. I'm done with him," Mrs. Fitz said, angrily folding her arms across her chest.

Berry leaned forward. "It's not Harry. It's Mildred and Bill—and Mrs. Dugan!"

"I got food poisoning," Mrs. Dugan explained, hanging her purse on the back of a chair. "Thought I was going to die. The ship company was real nice about it. They put me up in a hospital in Vancouver for two days and then flew me home. I tried calling last night from the airport, but there wasn't any answer at the house, and the Pizza Place line was always busy."

"So she called us," Mildred smiled. "Lucky we came home from our honeymoon early." She nudged Mrs. Dugan in the arm. "Tell them about Frank."

Mrs. Dugan poured herself a cup of tea. "Before I got sick I met the nicest man. He lives just blocks from here. Can you imagine that?"

"Has he got friends?" Mrs. Fitz asked. "I need a new boyfriend."

Bill helped himself to an English muffin. "Nicky Petrowski's going to be glad to hear that. He saw you at our party and thought you were really something."

Mrs. Fitz looked skeptical. "Nicky Petrowski. Was he the one with the tattoo on his forehead?"

"Naw, that's Bucky Weaver. He's missing a few marbles. I don't think you want to go out with Bucky Weaver. Nicky Petrowski's the one who can touch his nose with his tongue."

"I remember him. He's real cute," Mrs. Fitz said.

Berry glanced at the clock and drained her coffee cup. "I'd like to stay and hear more about Nicky Petrowski's tongue, but I've got to take an economics exam this morning."

"I'll drop you off at school," Jake said, taking a set of keys from the kitchen counter.

The drive to the college was quiet. Berry stared at her naked ring finger and wondered if she was still engaged. She was afraid to ask. What if he said no? She tilted her chin up a fraction of an inch. Then she'd make the best of it. Obviously, he enjoyed sleeping with her. If that was to be the extent of their relationship, she'd just have to go day by day and try to put limitations on her feelings. Lord, how did you do that when you were coconuts over someone? Maybe in time, she decided. Maybe after awhile his feelings would turn back to marriage. She clasped her hands together. It was going to hurt to have to wait. She wanted to be a permanent part of him now. There were things she had to share with him . . . silly jokes, comfortable silences, promotions, rejections, income tax audits, childbirth. Especially childbirth. She pressed her lips together and stole a brief glance at Jake. Ironic that she finally understood his impatience, just when he seemed to have adopted her reluctance.

Jake pulled to the curb and let the engine idle. A muscle worked in his jaw while he stared at the steering wheel.

Berry's stomach turned. This is it, she thought, barely able to breathe. He's going to dump me. This is the kiss-off. Good-bye, Berry, it's been fun.

"Berry, there's something I have to tell you . . ."

She was going to be sick. Or she was going to cry. Maybe she'd do both. Shape up, Berry, she ordered. You can't throw up in this car. It's a rental.

"You're as white as a sheet! Is it your stomach?" Jake asked hopefully, putting his hand to her forehead.

He sounded happy. Probably he'd go into ecstasy if she had dysentery. "It's my exam. I'm worried about my exam."

"Maybe we should talk later."

"Yeah, later would be better." Two hundred years later.

• • •

Berry skipped down the classroom building steps in a state of giddy euphoria. It was over, and she knew she'd passed both her exams with flying colors. If she took courses this summer, she'd be a senior in the fall.

A long arm reached out and snagged her by the elbow. "Whoa, where's the rush?"

Berry looked up to see Jake's brooding face. "I'm done. I passed. I know this sounds silly, but I felt like I needed to run."

The somber mood was instantly replaced with a smile that only partially reached his eyes. "That's great. I'm happy for you."

Berry clutched her books to her chest. "I suppose we have to talk now."

"I suppose we do." He plunged his hands into his pockets and studied his shoes. "I have some good news, and some bad news." He looked around. "Would you mind if we went back to the house where it's more private?"

She nodded and followed him to the car. *Well, phooey, so what if he gives me the old heave-ho. There are lots more where he came from.* She shook her head. *Berry, Berry, Berry. Who are you trying to kid? Like Mrs. Fitz said, after you've eaten breakfast with Jake Sawyer, you're ruined.*

"Where's the station wagon?" Berry said, shading her eyes from the sun, looking for the car.

"That's part of the good news. I bought a new car. What do you think?"

"This is your new car? This flashy red number? Wow, what is it?"

"It's a Ferrari."

Holy cow, a Ferrari. It looked like it should come equipped with James Bond. Berry slid into the passenger seat. Major depression. This was *not* a family car. He probably bought the darn thing with the money he got back from the ring. "Okay, let's go. Let's get to the house so I can hear the bad news. Boy, I can't wait. I love bad news."

Jake crept out into the afternoon traffic. "It's not such bad news. Good news and bad news is a figure of speech. Actually, the bad news is sort of boring. It's not worth getting upset over. Maybe it's the car that's upsetting you. Do you hate the car?"

"Are you kidding? How could anyone hate this car? This car is . . . nifty." Of course I hate the car, you insensitive bachelor, she thought. Why couldn't you buy a four-door sedan? You could put a pregnant wife and kids in a four-door sedan. Or better yet, station wagon. Then the dogs would fit. She folded her arms across her chest and slunk down in her seat, feeling numb. Tomorrow she would cry her eyes out and smash pizza dough until she was exhausted. It's not so bad, she told herself. You've been through this before. You know how to repair a broken heart and damaged ego.

Jake parked in the driveway and fiddled with his keys. He looked at the house and sighed. "The bad new is . . . the house still smells."

"That's the bad news?" Berry didn't know whether to scream, cry or burst out laughing. Get a grip, she told herself. You're getting hysterical.

"I know you're really ticked off about this smell business. It's just that I was in such a panic. I was so crazy in love with you that I couldn't think straight. All I knew was that I couldn't live without you. You made this big, empty house into a home. The minute you stepped through the door I could smell pudding cooking on the stove and hear kids running up and down the stairs. That was when I made up my plan. All I could think about, day and night, was having you by my side and buying a dog. I know it was dumb of me to rush out and buy Jane, but it symbolized commitment to me. I guess it was a way of reassuring myself that everything would work out . . . that you would be a permanent part of my life." He thumped the steering wheel. "Man, I really screwed this up. I just thought, maybe if you had longer to get to know me . . ." He turned and faced her. His finger trembled as it traced a whisper-soft line along her jaw. "Lord, Berry, I love you more than life itself. I know it makes you sick to your stomach to wear my ring, but—"

"*What?*"

"I'm willing to wait. We could live together for awhile. No pressure until you're ready. I promise I won't mention the ring again. We don't even have to have kids right away. We could get another dog." He saw the look of horror on her face and held up his hands. "Okay, no more dogs."

"Is this why you kept asking me about my stomach?"

"As soon as you got the ring off your finger, your stomach felt fine. Boy, talk about depressing."

A small nervous giggle escaped from Berry's lips. It turned into a chuckle and then she threw her head back and let great peals of laughter ripple through the air. She hugged Jake with all her strength and gave him a big smackeroo kiss square on the lips. She looked into his startled eyes and saw love shimmering there. "Boy, have I been dumb." She kissed him again. This time it was gentle and languorous. It said *I love you, I need you, I want to marry you.* "I have a lot of explaining to do, but first, I think I'm going to make love with you in this flashy car."

"It's not very big."

"It will be when I'm done with it."

Jake's eyes crinkled into laugh lines. "I meant the car."

"Of course. I knew that. Are you going to argue with me about this, or what?"

"I think I'm going to or what."

Half an hour later they rolled out of the car onto the grass and lay there in a fit of giggles.

"Well, we did it," Berry gasped, straightening her shirt.

"My back will never be the same. I think I'm too old for this car stuff."

"Now I can say I've been boinked in a Ferrari." Berry collapsed into another fit of giggles.

"Tonight I'm going to do it right—soft music, candles, satin sheets . . ."

"Sounds wonderful, but we have wall-to-wall ladies in my apartment."

"I never told you the rest of the good news. I've sold partial rights to a computer game I originally designed for my nephew. And next month United Foods will begin introducing an entire line of Jake's Junk. We're moderately rich. We can sleep wherever we want tonight. Juneau, Japan, the Grand Canyon." His eyes held hers in a silent affirmation of love. "I want to make things nice for you. If you want to finish school and be a pizza tycoon, that's fine. But I want to pamper you a little, too."

Berry lazily watched Jake reach into his jeans pocket and extract something that flashed in the waning sunlight. "My ring!"

"I've had it sterilized and sized." He slipped the ring on her finger. "This is just as binding as a marriage ceremony, Lingonberry Knudsen. I promise to love you forever and ever, good times, bad times, 'til death do us part."

"Till death do us part," she repeated. "Good times, bad times, love everlasting."

THE EDITOR'S CORNER

June is certainly a month for gorgeous, passionate, independent, loving, tender, daring, remarkable heroines! With three of the six women of the month being redheads, you can be sure to expect fireworks! Magdelena is washed right into her lover's arms in the rapids; Lux falls into her lover's arms with a giant teddy bear; Meghan has risky plans for her man; Candace finally wants to give all; Lacey's free spirit needs taming; and Randy learns to surrender . . . All this and a whole lot more in our June LOVESWEPTs. Read on to learn about each book and the wonderful heroes who fall in love with these six fabulous heroines.

In **CONFLICT OF INTEREST** by Margie McDonnell, LOVESWEPT #258, Magdelena Dailey, our heroine with long, wild hair, is rescued from a Colorado river by Joshua Wade who steals a passionate kiss as his reward. Joshua is a sweet seducer, a man made for love. Magdelena needs quite a bit of convincing before she changes her plans and lets a man into her life again, and Joshua is up to the challenge. There's no resisting his strong arms and tender smile, and soon Magdelena is riding the rapids of love!

Lux Sherwood is a raven-haired beauty in **WARM FUZZIES,** LOVESWEPT #259, by one of our perennial favorites, Joan Elliott Pickart. All Lux needs is one of her very own creations—a giant teddy bear—to get Patrick "Acer" Mullaney's attention. Acer is a star quarterback with a serious injury that's keeping him out of the game—the game of football, that is. He's definitely strong enough to participate in the game of love, and here's just a taste of what Acer has to say to Lux:

> "My needs run in a different direction. I need to kiss you, hold you, touch you. I need to make love to you until I'm too exhausted to move. I don't want to be just your friend, Lux. I won't be."

(continued)

What's a woman to say to such a declaration? Lux finds the right words, and the right actions in **WARM FUZZIES**!

We're so pleased to bring you our next LOVESWEPT for the month, **DIVINE DESIGN**, #260, by first novelist Mary Kay McComas. With a redheaded heroine like Meghan Shay and her daring scheme, we're certain that Mary Kay McComas is headed for LOVESWEPT success! Her hero in **DIVINE DESIGN** isn't bad either! Who can resist a long, tall Texan whose eyes gleam with intelligence *and* naked desire. Michael Ramsey has all the qualifications that Meghan is looking for—in fact he's too perfect, too good looking, too kind, too wonderful—and she can't help but fall in love, and that's not part of Meghan's plans. Ah, the best laid plans . . .

Barbara Boswell delivers another moving love story with **BABY, BABY,** LOVESWEPT #261. By popular demand, Barbara brings you Candace "Barracuda" Flynn's love story. And what a love story it is! Candace wants a second chance with Nick Torcia, but Nick is wary—as well he should be. Candace burned him once, and he isn't coming back for more. But something has changed. Precious new babies have brought them both an understanding of love. Still, Nick needs to lay the past to rest. Here's a sample of the intensity of their encounter:

> "Why did you lead me on, Candy?" Nick demanded, his onyx eyes burning into hers.
>
> "Not for revenge," she whispered.
>
> "Then why, Candy?"
>
> Her heart seemed to stop beating. He was so close to her, close enough for her to feel the heat emanating from his hard, masculine frame.
>
> "Nick." His name escaped from her throat in a husky whisper, and she tried to move closer. Desire, sharp as a stiletto, sliced through her. She wanted to lose herself in his arms, to feel his hot, hard mouth take hers. She gazed at him with undisguised yearning.
>
> But Nick wouldn't let her close the gap between them. He held her wrists, controlling her movements and keeping her anchored in place. "Tell me, Candy."

Tyler Winter is the man who tames Lacey Lee Wilcox's free spirit in **FOR THE LOVE OF LACEY**, LOVESWEPT #262, by Sandra Chastain. Tyler is a renaissance man—an artist, businessman, and an absolutely irresistible hunk! Is

(continued)

he a flirt or really a man Lacey can trust her heart to? Tyler showers her with kisses, gives her wildflowers, and takes her on picnics, but still Lacey is afraid of losing her heart. With just a little more convincing our heroine loses her fears and listens to her heart:

"Tyler, turn me loose," Lacey ordered.

"Nope," he said, moving his mouth toward hers.

Not again, she begged silently. Too late. She was being kissed, thoroughly kissed, and there was no way to stop him. Tyler finally drew back and grinned down at her with undisguised joy.

"Tyler," she protested, "you don't know what you're doing."

"You're right, and it's been a long time since ignorance felt so good. Kiss me, Lacey."

In **HAWK O'TOOLE'S HOSTAGE** by Sandra Brown, LOVESWEPT #263, Randy Price can't believe what's happening to her. It's 1987, yet she's just been abducted by a masked man on a horse! No, this is not part of the old west show she was watching with her son. Who is this masked man? And why does he want Randy? Hawk O'Toole is an Indian Chief with very good and honorable reasons for kidnapping Randy Price, but he doesn't plan on the intense attraction he feels toward her. She's his hostage, but fate turns the tables, and he becomes her slave. Love has a way of quieting the fiercest battles as Randy and Hawk find out.

Happy Reading! Remember to look for The Hometown Hunk Contest next month—it's your big chance to find the perfect LOVESWEPT hero!

Sincerely,

Kate Hartson

Kate Hartson
    Editor

LOVESWEPT
Bantam Books.
666 Fifth Avenue
New York, NY 10103

ENTER
THE DELANEYS, THE UNTAMED YEARS
MISSISSIPPI QUEEN' RIVERBOAT CRUISE
SWEEPSTAKES
W I N
7 NIGHTS ABOARD THE LUXURIOUS
MISSISSIPPI QUEEN STEAMBOAT
including double occupancy accommodations,
meals and fabulous entertainment for two

She's elegant. Regal. Alive with music and moonlight. You'll find
a Jacuzzi, gym, sauna, movie theatre, gift shop, library, beauty
salon and multi-tiered sun deck aboard…plus a splendid dining
room and lounges, beveled mirrors, polished brass, a Grand
Saloon where big band sounds soothe your soul and set your feet
to dancing! For further information and/or reservations on the
Mississippi Queen and Delta Queen' Steamboats
CALL 1-800-458-6789!

Sweepstakes travel arrangements by
RELIABLE TRAVEL INTERNATIONAL, INC.

RELIABLE TRAVEL INTERNATIONAL, INC.

Whether you're travelling for business, romance or adventure,
you're a winner with Reliable Travel International!
CALL TOLL FREE FOR INFORMATION AND RESERVATIONS
1-800-645-6504 Ext. 413

**MISSISSIPPI QUEEN RIVERBOAT CRUISE SWEEPSTAKES
RULES AND ENTRY FORMS ALSO APPEAR IN THE
FOLLOWING BANTAM <u>LOVESWEPT</u> NOVELS:**

THE GRAND FINALE	MAN FROM HALF MOON BAY
HOLD ON TIGHT	OUTLAW DEREK
*CONFLICT OF INTEREST	*DIVINE DESIGN
*WARM FUZZIES	*BABY, BABY
*FOR LOVE OF LACEY	*HAWK O'TOOLE'S HOSTAGE

and in

**THE DELANEYS, THE UNTAMED YEARS:
COPPER FIRE; WILD SILVER; GOLDEN FLAMES**

*On sale week of May 2, 1988   SW'10

OFFICIAL DELANEYS, THE UNTAMED YEARS
MISSISSIPPI QUEEN' RIVERBOAT CRUISE
SWEEPSTAKES RULES

1. NO PURCHASE NECESSARY. Enter by completing the Official Entry Form below (or print your name, address, date of birth and telephone number on a plain 3"x 5" card) and send to:

> Bantam Books
> Delaneys, THE UNTAMED YEARS Sweepstakes
> Dept. HBG
> 666 Fifth Avenue
> New York, NY 10103

2. One Grand Prize will be awarded. There will be no prize substitutions or cash equivalents permitted. Grand Prize is a 7-night riverboat cruise for two on the luxury steamboat, The Mississippi Queen. Double occupancy accommodations, meals and on-board entertainment included. Round trip airfare provided by Reliable Travel International, Inc. (Estimated retail value $5,500.00. Exact value depends on actual point of departure.)

3. All entries must be postmarked and received by Bantam Books no later than August 1, 1988. The winner, chosen by random drawing, will be announced and notified by November 30, 1988. Trip must be completed by December 31, 1989, and is subject to space availability determined by Delta Queen Steamboat Company, and airline space availability determined by Reliable Travel International. If the Grand Prize winner is under 21 years of age on August 1, 1988, he/she must be accompanied by a parent or guardian. Taxes on the prize are the sole responsibility of the winner. Odds of winning depend on the number of completed entries received. Enter as often as you wish, but each entry must be mailed separately. Bantam Books is not responsible for lost, misdirected or incomplete entries.

4. The sweepstakes is open to residents of the U.S. and Canada, except the Province of Quebec, and is void where prohibited by law. If the winner is a Canadian he/she will be required to correctly answer a skill question in order to receive the prize. All federal, state and local regulations apply. Employees of Reliable Travel International, The Delta Queen Steamboat Co., and Bantam, Doubleday, Dell Publishing Group, Inc., their subsidiary and affiliates, and their immediate families are ineligible to enter.

5. The winner may be required to submit an Affidavit of Eligibility and Promotional Release supplied by Bantam Books. The winner's name and likeness may be used for publicity purposes without additional compensation.

6. For an extra copy of the Official Rules and Entry Form, send a self-addressed stamped envelope (Washington and Vermont Residents need not affix postage) by June 15, 1988 to:

> Bantam Books
> Delaneys, THE UNTAMED YEARS Sweepstakes
> Dept. HBG
> 666 Fifth Avenue
> New York, NY 10103

OFFICIAL ENTRY FORM
DELANEYS, THE UNTAMED YEARS
MISSISSIPPI QUEEN' RIVERBOAT CRUISE SWEEPSTAKES

Name_____

Address _____

City_____ State_____ Zip Code_____

SW10